John Newton's Short Stories

First published in paperback in The United Kingdom by Next Century Books, December 2023

Reprinted May 2024.

Cover Design and Layout by John Newton and James Harvey

Printed and bound in The UK by
P2D Books Ltd
Westoning, Bedfordshire, MK45 5LD

ISBN 9781739530839

Contents

Hook Line and Sinker

A summer's day came. Carrying chilled Bollinger and two champagne flutes I trod the Riviera Beach seeking a target.

I'd call myself a gigolo if I knew how to say it, but I've been through a dull patch. My last pickup saw through my rough-boy-trader-down-on-his-luck act in only three days and threw me out before I could tap her for cash.

So, struggling on my last thousand I decided this time to be the suave, sophisticated financier. Hence the Bolly, the flutes, and the swish new show-off rich-young-man outfit, with my tanned and slightly oiled muscles gleaming in the sun.

Plenty of eyes fluttered in my direction from topless beach dollies with no obvious means of support. Financial support that is. Sorry girls. Its money I'm after.

Finally, I caught a glance from a good prospect; not quite middle-aged, not quite beautiful, but draped across the sand in an expensive flowered one piece, fingers twinkling with diamonds.

I looked. She smiled. I winked.

'Do you accept champagne from strangers?'

'Only the best.'

She patted. I sat. We sipped Bollinger and chatted.

By sunset we were friends, by midnight lovers.

She'd taken the hook.

In her luxury villa we slept on silken sheets; dined cordon bleu and talked and talked and talked for a week.

She told me of her late husband's great wealth.

I told her of my many big deals round the world.

Eyes sparkling, she showed great interest. I'll soon tighten the line, reel her in and cash will come to Daddy.

One idyllic evening – a fragrant cliff top restaurant; dinner and champagne under the stars – I twitched the line.

'One of my big projects is giving trouble, darling. I'm piled up at the banks and need short term finance. Can you help?'

'How much?'

'Quarter of a million.'

'A lot of money.'

'Yes, but your husband left you a fortune.'

'No. Neither my husband nor his money exist.'

A shocked pause.

'Don't exist? What do you mean? What about the diamonds, the villa?'

She looked deep into my eyes, held my hand, and whispered, 'Oh my sweet darling. Like both of us they're fake. We're in the same game. I extract money from rich handsome men then disappear. I planned to tap you this evening. What perfect timing. We're trying to con each other.'

Her eyes filled with tears, 'What will you do now?'

Oh my God. What can I do? I've fallen in love with the damned woman. She's hooked me.

She brushed my cheek with a kiss and murmured, 'Trouble is, I have fallen in love with you. Please don't leave.'

She wept. I cried. We embraced. The Maitre, convinced I'd popped the question, sent across flowers and a violinist.

So, what did we do?

In a close and loving partnership, we spent four years conning cash from elderly businessmen before retiring from crime and opening an honest business.

I won't tell you what business but promise it is honest. Well, almost honest.

Honestly.

Madame Sinskaya And The Largest Anthology In History

Around the time of my fourth birthday my mother became certain she had produced a writing genius and started to tell all her friends in great detail. It became apparent to me at the age of eight that Mother's previous friends no longer called and scampered across the road or into shops to avoid forced recitations of my latest intellectual exploit.

I recognised these people as small-minded and by the age of ten felt ready to submit stories and articles to magazines and agents. At school I became known as a great English student and writer and knowledgeable at everything except maths, science, geography, history, languages, woodwork, and games.

Nevertheless, I gave teachers and fellow pupils the benefit of my research in all these subjects and many more until, at the age of fifteen the head confirmed my brilliance with a letter to Mother saying, "It seems we really cannot teach this boy anything he does not already know. He is wasting our time and therefore must leave this school."

Encouraged by such excellent endorsement I settled to write and write and write. I continued until the age of eighteen, during which time editors and agents, whilst expressing admiration

at my abilities and skill, found themselves unable to accept my work. I agreed with Mother that they were also small-minded and unable to trust the brilliance of one so young, fearing I may burn out early, so I set the many rejected works aside for inclusion in the inevitable Anthology once I became famous.

To gain insight in story structures and marketing I joined a writing school run by the famous Madame Sinskaya, a tall, stately lady topped by a well-constructed hairstyle that climbed a further six precarious inches. Strong and wide at shoulder and hip and dressed always in flowing silk, she moved with all the grace and care of a clipper ship entering harbour, her arrival at class preceded by a bow wave of expensive perfume.

I soon noticed that all students accepted by Madame Sinskaya – whatever their standard of education or writing skills – were well built young men. It seemed that girls or women who applied to join always failed the first interview.

Confiding one day that she had been born a White Russian gave me a story idea. Poor teaching at school left me unable to remember anything about that country but from her reference to colour I assumed that Russians came in varying shades from white through purple, yellow, and magenta to black. So, I plucked a likely shade from the rainbow and wrote a piece about Red Russians who overthrew the government and ruled by fear, forcing all White Russians out and enslaving the rest.

My story had an astonishing effect on Madame Sinskaya. Reading the piece aloud in class she wept and wailed, 'Look at how this young man understands my country. Oh, my dear boy, your research is perfect, and you tell exactly what happened.' To my surprise she hurried across the room, lifted me from my seat and pulled me into an enormous hug.

Previous warnings of Madame Sinskaya's hugs left me unprepared for an experience akin to being strapped by steel wires to tall soft pillow. I cannot describe the strength of the woman's arms. From then on she found every excuse to hug me in class, in the corridor and eventually in a small cupboard under the stairs. I ignored sarcasm from other students at gaining extraordinarily high marks for whatever I wrote thereafter, recognising it as jealousy for genius. Eventually I left the school, feeling Madame Sinskaya could teach me nothing about writing although, for a time, I did miss that small cupboard under the stairs.

I settled in a garret to write and starve, both of which I found easy. I set all my work from Madame Sinskaya's aside for my eventual Anthology and wrote several dozen novels all of which were received with great enthusiasm by agents and publishers who wrote rejection letters in glowing terms.

One especially appreciative publisher, referring to my short novel about bullying in a 19th century boys' school, enthused at what he called, "The finest and most detailed example of high-class plagiarism I have ever encountered. The idea of calling the book John Brown's Schooldays is a masterstroke that underlines the standard of the whole work."

I treasure this letter and plan to include it prominently in my Anthology alongside the actual book as truly wonderful approval of my work.

After a year, both garret and starvation lost appeal, so I tried making money by writing advertising jingles and slogans. Based on memories of my hypochondriac grandmother, I devised a cleverly constructed marketing campaign for international drug companies and met with enormous success. First I set up a contact club called Hypochondria International with the slogan Hypochondriacs Of The World – Unite! Applications flooded in from all over the world, many with heart-rending letters pleading for vaguely described ailments to be understood.

This brought the idea that made my fortune – Hypochondriacs Reunited – which allows all those who think they are ill to meet like-minded people on the Internet to swap symptoms and convince themselves they are ill. The resulting worldwide sales surge of proprietary drugs – for which I previously negotiated a first-class commission – brought riches to both the drug companies and to me.

A year or two after leaving garret and starvation I bumped into Madame Sinskaya as she navigated a street corner under full sail. She hove to and pulled me with wire hawser arms into one of her huge hugs, breathing husky welcome while covering my cheeks with damp kisses. 'Oh, my lovely boy, you were always my lovely boy,' she murmured. 'Come home and join me for tea.' Strapped so tight to her pillow-soft front I found no breath to refuse so she whisked me by taxi to an enormous mansion, purchased, she said, with inheritance from her late White Russian Royal Duke husband.

It seems she now owned many millions in jewels and paintings recovered from Nazis or Communists or some such and had abandoned literary teaching. I found her attractions greatly improved by these new circumstances and sat late into the evening comparing bank balances.

Hers turned out far greater than mine, so I mentioned only the garret and the starvation and agreed to her kind offer to be rescued and to stay and settle with her in this fine mansion. 'You'll have all the time in the world to write, my lovely boy,' she gushed, 'and you can help me look after all my money, because I don't really understand it.'

So now I spend time being hugged but much more time secretly moving my drug company commissions round international banks and siphoning portions of Madame Sinskaya's profits in the same direction, all the time blessing my luck and the writing skills that brought me to such comfort and security. I continue, without Madame Sinskaya noticing, to run both Hypochondriacs International and Reunited and write the occasional new novel.

But my main literary effort is directed at gathering together my large body of unpublished work into what will probably become the Largest Anthology In History.

I also plan a separate book containing my glowing and congratulatory rejection letters to show new aspiring writers what can be achieved through hard work and application. Madame Sinskaya - besotted as always - insists on financing my Anthology. The title? Ah yes, the title. My Anthology will be called, 'Oh The Joys Of Writing'. Quite apt don't you think?

Dead Silence

My mother cuddled her beautiful newly born little girl without realising she had brought me into the world without hearing of any kind.

'It must be a genetic condition, passed down in families,' said several experts.

'But we have no history of deafness in our family,' protested my mother, many times.

'Then it's from your husband's side,' said the clinicians. 'Nothing we can do. You'll have to live with it.'

'Not me,' said Mother. 'You are talking about my daughter. She'll have to live with it.'

I grew up in dead silence, never hearing my mother's voice; never hearing the wind or dogs barking or birdsong or music or the voices of friends and relatives, or the many sounds of nature that I understand make life so magnificent. And, of course, I never learned to speak,

Growing up I let nothing stand in my way. At a special school I learned the use of movements of my hands, body, face, and head to express myself. And, when needed, used a pen and pad to write questions and answers.

I became so proficient that, by the age of twenty, I began teaching at a special unit for children with the same affliction. I fell in love with the unit leader, a handsome young man of full hearing and speech and a renowned specialist in sign language.

After several years happy marriage filled with love, laughter and long, signed conversations, he stood up at dinner in a restaurant and signed, 'Only be a minute.'

But he never came back.

The police came with a sign language interpreter and asked me many questions. "Has he done this before?'

I tapped two fingers to thumb to say, 'No.'

'Have you any idea why he should go?'

'No.'

'Describe him.'

I fingered his name and signed a detailed description with both hands moving at speed, followed by a history of our time together and they took me home to my empty house.

Neither of us had family I could turn to so I remained at the school and continued teaching.

For three years I searched, wrote letters, used private detectives and various authorities to check ports and airports, hotels and holiday destinations in my hunting for the man I loved and married. Many tear-stained letters went out across many countries. The internet proved useless. I had plenty of sympathy and offers of suspicious companionship from both men and women, including marriage.

For three years I wept each night in my lonely bed, remembering 'Back in a minute.'

My loving husband had disappeared completely. After five years I gave up the search, stopped weeping and divorced him using a presumption of disappearance or death and married a lovely man with full speech and hearing. To make our life complete he learned sign language and we started our wonderful life together.

One sun-filled holiday on a Sardinian beach, I studied through binoculars a graceful yacht sailing in light winds on impossibly blue sea.

I turned my gaze to move slowly along the waterline at the bronzed young bodies in tiny trunks or almost invisible bikinis, when I saw him. My first husband. Walking hand in hand with a typical Italian beach beauty. Long black hair, flawless golden skin, a body of perfection barely covered by a few expensive strips of bright material.

He walked and whispered.

She rubbed against him, nodding; small subtle smiles flicking across immaculate pouting lips.

Jealously gripped my heart.

I must have grunted my surprise.

Fingers tapped my shoulder.

"Are you ok?' signed my lovely but now illegal second husband.

I nodded.

'Perfect.' I replied.

I looked again and decided to let the finding of my first husband pass.

If I don't I'll be a bigamist.

Forget the crushing burden of abandonment. Forget the years of tears. Forget the treacherous bastard. Let him go to hell. For ever.

Let little Miss Perfect have him.

I'll keep dead silent and stick with this one. s

Freddie, the Mafia Man

Forty years of travel round the world in some very odd places I met and made friends with some very odd people. One of the more absorbing is Freddie Markus, the Mafia man. Despite being Canadian, he really had been a member of the Mafia. Honest.

Here in quiet little England, it may be difficult to believe but, the contact came from our Orange Juice suppliers in Israel, a factory named Jafora. It seems that Ed had married an Israeli woman. She lived in Israel, but, although also Jewish, he didn't, for reasons that will become apparent.

Ed came to London and started a business called Mr Pizza Man. He needed a source of inexpensive pizza sauce and his wife approached Jafora, whose deputy managing director, Yigal Carmil, met Ed at a trade show in Europe and was bowled over by his charm and wit. Yigal is as naïve as a puppy and Ed, a practised con man, knew exactly how to tickle Yigal's tummy, resulting in Yigal contacting me and asking us to import and sell a planned twenty to fifty loads of pizza sauce a year to Freddie and his new business. At around thirty thousand dollars a load this seemed an attractive deal.

In America it is generally known that the US pizza sauce business, based around Chicago, is very much controlled by the Mafia of that area and their grip on the product runs throughout The States and Canada. Shortly after my discussion with Yigal I saw a copy of an article from Private Eye describing Ed and his new business in detail, the main thrust being that Ed was recently released from a five-year jail term in New York for selling American investors non-existent orange groves in Brazil. Ed's victims found no redress in the arrest since he had tied up the money gained in long-term bonds, impossible to break. The article made no mention of the Mafia.

I sent Yigal a copy of the article but – tummy still tingling with pleasure – he refused to believe that Freddie was anything but completely reformed. 'When you meet him, you will see, John. He is a lovely man with a lovely wife living here in Tel Aviv. Ed told me all about his past, and promises he is reformed and trying to go straight with this new business. His wife has given us all guarantees and I believe in them both.'

Ho-ho. Is this true? Well now, a few days later The Sunday Times wrote a much more penetrating article about Freddie. No doubt sparked off by the Private Eye piece it went over the same ground but stated categorically that Freddie had direct Mafia links both to Chicago and elsewhere and gave a specific example. You may remember Meyer Lansky, the Jewish American who acted as banker to the main Mafia families in the US and became the prime mover in the attempt to buy the government of Cuba from Fulgencio Batista, the then Cuban dictator. You may also remember that Lansky, after a lifetime of crime, finally fled to Israel under the Right of Return to avoid US charges of racketeering that would have placed him in prison for the rest of his life.

The Sunday Times said that Ed, looking for finance for some scam or other, flew to Israel trying to meet with Lansky and ask his assistance. But the Israeli police already knew of the trip and despite Ed's wife's Tel Aviv domicile and although Ed, being Jewish, could claim full Right of Return, the immigration and police refused entry and hustled him back onto the plane to the USA.

I sent the article to Yigal who STILL swore that Freddie had reformed and is a good guy. At Yigal's suggestion I went to London and met Ed in his factory – a well set up modern operation with excellent equipment. I must say that Freddie certainly knew how to sell pizza and seemed to be doing well. But meeting the man with eyes opened by the two articles one could look behind the extreme charm, the immediate friendly welcome and big smile; the arm round the shoulders; the expert schmoozing. I think I may have been wary without the articles, but with them...

His office seemed as false as his smile. No business paper or invoices. No sign of any accounts or accountant. No feeling that this had anything to do with business. Instead, it seemed to be a sort of clubroom; filled with framed, almost certainly doctored, photos of Freddie on the golf course, shaking hands with celebrities, or in a tuxedo with a group of rich men and their wives, some of whom looked vaguely familiar. And in the corner a set of golf clubs, balls, and a putting practise cup. It seemed to me to be a staged film-set office. No work, no perspiration. Only entertainment.

We chatted and I asked him about the damaging articles. 'Old hat and all over. I'm reformed,' said Ed with outstretched arms and a rueful expression 'I don't do that stuff anymore.'

I came away unconvinced and told Yigal, 'We will act only as commission agent. The deal is direct between Freddie and Jafora with us merely helping with importing and paperwork for a fee.'

I took this line partly because I checked through a couple of banks on Freddie's financial operation. It turned out that hardly any of the money generated by this cash-only business stayed in Mr Pizza Man, most being shipped daily to an anonymous account in a small bank in the Irish Republic. From there it disappeared to heaven knows where.

We ran the business for about a year on this basis before Freddie just disappeared leaving about fifteen loads - half a million dollars - unpaid. Because, although the original deal insisted that Freddie pay on delivery, as time went by, he slipped back with excuses and sweet words to Yigal, with me saying, 'Yigal, you've had your tummy tickled again,'

Jafora allowed Freddie this creeping credit until he skipped and left them dry. Off he went. No forwarding address. No goodbye. Not even a casual wave as he followed his money via Ireland, probably to some prepared bolthole where he could hide and plan his next scam.

There are two sequels. The first occurred a year later when Pam and I were on holiday in America and stayed the night at Bakersfield. We wandered into a book- shop and I chanced upon a biography of Meyer Lansky, the Mafia banker. Wondering if the stories about Ed were true, I looked through the index for 'Markus' and there he was. I checked the page, and it confirmed the story of Ed trying to enter Israel to meet Lansky and being chucked out. I felt so excited I shouted across the shop to Pam, 'Freddie is in this book,' and felt vindicated in believing the original Private Eye article.

The second happened in my Leighton Buzzard office. I read a short piece in The Sunday Times that mentioned Freddie Markus, "subject of previous Sunday Times investigations", had been jailed for six years in Amsterdam for a diamond fraud. No money from that fraud had been recovered his pension seemed still intact.

I could not resist writing to Freddie, care of the Dutch Prison Service in Amsterdam. I expressed pleasure at hearing of him again and repeated what I'd once said to his face: 'You are so clever it is a pity you're not straight. With your brain and charm, you'd make a first-class politician. You could easily run a country.' He'd laughed and said, 'Difficult, because really I'm a criminal at heart. I'm just naturally bent.' I also said in my letter, 'Since you seem to have the diamond money tucked safely away, why can't you be decent and send some of it to Yigal for the pizza sauce you never paid for?'

I thought that would be that, but do you know, about three weeks later Freddie telephoned our office from prison in Amsterdam. Unfortunately, being out, he spoke to Pam and said, 'Tell John Newton I am not the Ed Markus he thinks. I do not know John Newton and have never met him. Tell him not to contact me again and tell him he will never hear from me again.'

He spoke quite politely and without menace, but Pam recognised his voice and said along the lines of, 'Okay Freddie. I'll tell him.' And that ended that. I never felt threatened and never heard from him again.

Conspiracy

I kept my eye firmly on my Mark trying to disappear in the throng of office workers pushing over London Bridge towards Westminster. I'd been tracking him for almost an hour and must not lose him now. He may know or feel he is being followed.

My Lamplighter across the road probably sensed my worry. 'I've got him clocked,' he whispered into my earpiece. It's the pink socks. Can't miss 'em. I think he's edging towards Parliament.'

But the man turned right and into Whitehall before stopping by a small café to study the menu. A young woman stepped into the street. After a few words my Mark handed her a small package and walked on.

Lucky I'd thought of bringing backup. 'You follow the bloke,' I told him. 'I want to see where the package goes.'

Across the street my Lamplighter touched his nose in agreement. The woman, small, pretty and looking as innocent as an angel, slipped back into the café.

I followed and took a window seat to watch both the street and the woman, noting that she sat in a corner with her back to the wall, the classic position of a well-trained operative. She may not, after all, be an angel.

Sipping her coffee with one hand, she slipped the package into her bag with the other, not giving anything away by checking around for watchers. She must be well trained and confident.

She placed the bag on the floor. Another, older woman, entered and took the next table and placed a precisely similar bag alongside. They did not look at each other, but the older woman took out a diary, made an act of checking and realising in horror that she must be somewhere else, grabbed the wrong bag and rushed from the café.

Luck went my way. Two elderly couples, chatting and laughing, left their table and pushed out onto the street. Knowing that my young woman would not notice in the general hubbub, I jumped up and followed,

I saw my Lamplighter walking towards me. 'He's Russian,' my earpiece whispered. 'He went into the embassy.

'The girl's still in the café,' I said. 'Call Plod and pick her up.'

My new Mark clipped along on high heels. Not so well trained she didn't check for a follower until entering a park. She sat on a bench watching the entrance. I continued straight past with the fast walk of an important man. So many of those around this area, she wouldn't have noticed.

Flagging down a police car and flashing my warrant I said, 'I need three plain clothes here fast,' I said. 'If necessary, go and fetch them.'

I returned to the park through another gate. The car returned with three smallish men, not obvious bulky coppers. One carried a briefcase. Three businessmen looking to find somewhere for a crafty smoke. Someone had used their head.

'Get across to that bench, light up and be ready to snaffle whoever turns up and takes something from that woman,' I said. 'Wait until she's handed it to him and bring her along too.'

Within two minutes a middle-aged man turned up. He sat by the woman who showed all the anxious delight of welcoming a lover. They leaned against each other and hugged. She whipped the package from her bag and into his jacket pocket in mid-clinch. A passer-by would not have noticed. She'd probably been practicing for a week.

I nodded. My men moved in. The couple came without fuss and went into adjoining interview rooms. Both confessed.

The package went to forensics who found it held a small bottle of one of those poisons used by the Russians, identified in court as "Probably derived from the nerve agent Novichok. A ferocious killer."

The Commissioner called me in. 'We can never identify you, Superintendent, but you probably saved several lives and broke up a conspiracy to murder.'

We smiled and shook hands.

I left his office feeling very pleased with myself.

Another tick in my move towards promotion and a bigger pension.

The Dummy

Massachusetts Colony – 1692

John Proctor of Salem rose from his bed and dressed formally in dark Puritan attire of black coat, black breeches and tall black hat pushed firmly down on his thick black hair.

Checking in the small mirror hanging from a nail, he saw a middle-aged man dressed right and proper for the grim task ahead. He knew today would be difficult but felt ready to do his religious duty and sentence three women and one man to death for witchcraft and sorcery. The evidence had been clear, with flying dogs, talking pigs and one woman jumping over a house in full view of her neighbour.

Tweaking an errant strand of hair back into place, he cocked an ear to the clacking sound of wood on wood.

He opened the door, stepped out into unseasonable October frost and felt great surprise at seeing a Dummy or Puppet sitting on his rocking chair, somehow snapping its lower jaw against its upper mandible without sign or hint of any machine to make it so.

Checking around for strings or handles by which it could be operated and finding none, he stepped back to study the thing. Its doll face, badly carved in wood by some hand without skill, one shiny red cheek ballooned out twice as large as the other and the builder of this trifle could neither paint nor decorate in harmony. Both eyes, one large, round and green, the other a mean red slit, stared from under a jet-black slash of eyebrow.

The body, although dressed as an Indian, seemed no better built, with misshapen shoulders and varied unpainted twigs for arms, legs, toes and fingers.

The lower jaw continued clicking uneven white teeth up and down against equally uneven yellow teeth.

'Well, little man,' said Proctor with a chuckle. 'Who brought thee here? God or man?'

'Neither' hissed a voice in his head. 'My master, the Devil sent me to attend your court. I command you to pick me up, tuck me in your coat and carry me thence.'

Strangely unable to resist, Proctor picked the thing up and made his way, as though in a dream, to the crowded courtroom.

When Proctor stepped in the place fell silent and all eyes turned upon him. Henry Winter, senior judge, jumped to his feet, pointing with a quivering finger and shouted, 'Arrest that man. Proctor, thou art denounced as a witch and sorcerer. It is you who caused our harvest to fail.'

Proctor, struggling hard against the firm grip of three wardens dragging him to the stocks, felt the

Dummy slip from his coat. It fell to the floor, wriggled a few times, clacked its jaws and fell silent.

Barely heard above the awful moan that rose from court congregation, Winter, in quivering voice, cried, 'With this foul Satanic Doll, thou hast proved thy guilt as an agent of the Devil.'

The Dummy whispered, 'He's right. You are now truly an agent of my Master, the Devil.'

Shocked and unable to speak, Proctor heard himself condemned to burn in the fires of hell. Strapped to the post, with The Dummy tied around his neck, he felt no pain as flames rose and took hold, first on his lower legs, then up his body to set his face and hair alight.

The Dummy, also burning, whispered, 'As a servant of my Master, you will die without agony. Your revenge upon Martin and this place is that within a month he will die from a terrible illness and deep winter will fall and many will die from cold and starvation. Martin's last words will be to curse you and your Devil's Doll. Now you can die happy.

The Western Front – July 1916

A young Soldier dressed in a filthy mud and dirt-covered Bavarian Regiment uniform climbed the ladder of a small observation platform and squinted to stare across the familiar mud and shell holes of shattered landscape. Between the trench lines he could see columns of English troops marching to positions this side of that stupid little Somme River. He pulled nervously at the tips of the large moustache curving from upper lip to cheekbones.

So, the rumours must be correct. The damned enemy are preparing a big push. Thank God I'm stationed two kilometres behind the lines.

He heard the Major call and scrambled down to the roughly built lean-to serving as Company Headquarters. The Major handed him an envelope and said, 'Get this fast as possible to our machine guns' commander.'

The Soldier took the message and snapped a brisk salute, his arm sweeping up and over. His muddy jacket fell open and the brightly painted head of a small wooden Dummy popped out.

In obvious fury the Major shouted, 'Get rid of that Devilish Doll before you return. If you bring it back, I'll throw onto the cooking fire.'

'Aber mein Herr, he is my little Dummy-Puppe. He is my friend and lucky charm.'

'A stupid thing for a Soldier to carry. Stamp it into a mud hole or it burns.'

The Soldier pushed his Dummy back into place and ran from the lean-to. He had raced only a hundred metres when an English shell flew over his head into a direct hit on the lean-to.

Running back to help, the Soldier found his comrades shaken but safe. Except for the Major who lay in several pieces inside and around a small shell hole.

The Soldier turned and ran to deliver his message. The English began a continuous heavy barrage. The Soldier ducked behind a wall and took out his perfectly carved little Doll. Dressed in neat Bavarian jacket and lederhosen with green hat and feather perched on his head, the Dummy clicked its jaws in a happy tattoo.

'You got the bastard,' said the Soldier.

He straightened the Puppet's hat and smoothed the immaculate bristle moustache set under the handsomely chiselled nose. How smart. Perhaps I should trim mine to this shape.

The Soldier said, 'Why do shells never kill me and why am I never hit by bullets? Are you really my lucky charm? Why do you keep me safe?'

The sweetly toned voice he heard from time to time, whispered in his head.

'I keep you safe, Adolf, because my Master plans a great future for you.'

North Africa – Last Week.

Sitting in a small military vehicle on hills above the town, the Emir surveyed his Jihadists blowing up the final few buildings and beheading a dozen or so inhabitants in the main square.

Looking down at the badly carved Dummy dressed in Arab robes and kufiyah, the Emir said, 'I have won again. How many more great victories do I enjoy before ruling the world, Shaitan?'

The jaws of the Dummy clicked and clattered.

'None,' came a malevolent murmur in the Emir's head. 'My Master is consumed by jealousy that you and I have become more evil than he. And he dislikes you calling me his name. So, this is our end. You must now feel the fires of Hell and I must be scattered in splinters across the desert. Right now.'

A Hellfire missile whispered from the sky and landed directly on the Emir and his vile Dummy without giving the Emir even a second to wonder why Allah had abandoned him.

Dinner With Alice

Posted suddenly I travelled in my Land Rover up twisting dirt roads of the Rift Valley escarpment and arrived at Pencil Slats, my new police post after dark. Next morning, I stood enthralled in crisp clean highlands air to watch beautiful dawn creep across the vast plateau. Sunrise sparked off clear white snow capping Mount Kenya and in one exhilarating moment, I fell in love with the place.

My unexpected home seemed a concoction of old bits of wood held together by rusty nails and mud. A year ago, my predecessor struggled up in a lorry loaded with ancient planks twenty police askaris and a couple of hammers to nail the whole lot together. The askaris shoved up the walls, filled in the cracks then balanced a sloping tin roof. They banded and ringed the contraption with barbed wire and formed three small cages to act as cells. It seems haphazard but in those early days of The Emergency, a chain of police posts needed right across the highlands, were built any old how. Mine seemed typical; dumped on a patch of flat earth between the Aberdare forest and Laikipia plateau farmland stretching across to Mount Kenya.

My predecessor, taken suddenly ill, had been rushed down the escarpment several days before, leaving a sheaf of well-written notes and a neat incident book.

I spent several careful days planning how to run my two thousand square mile policing area then set off on a series of four-day Land Rover safaris along dirt roads, farm tracks and dangerous narrow trails zigzagging up and down forest escarpments. Taking two askaris and my cook I visited European farms across the plateau and African villages along the forest edge. Exhilarated and entranced by beautiful days, clear cold nights and the thrill of camping under black star-sparkled skies, I almost regretted time spent under a roof at my police post.

The strong-minded European farmers, well-armed and able to defend themselves against night-roaming terrorist gangs slinking from the forest seemed more worried by marauding elephant. One said, 'At least terrorists don't destroy our crops and we can shoot the buggers. Pop off at a damned elephant and you're straight into jail.' On the other hand, African villages, surrounded by deep ditches lined with sharpened stakes, were possible havens for forest gangs. I sat many hours debating security with Kikuyu elders, promising regular patrols and night ambushes.

I patrolled the far reaches of my area for almost three months, leaving nearer patrols to my Nandi sergeant, who never mentioned a European woman living alone nearby and I found Alice by chance.

On a dirt road ten miles from home, I almost missed a tiny name-board half hidden in long grass. It announced, 'The de Courcey Estate. Keep Out!' I turned into a lane so narrow my Land Rover barely scraped between thick bush scratching and squealing along my paintwork. After half a mile I entered a large area of well-tended lawn, dominated by a typical upcountry Kenya farmhouse – low slung, built mainly of wood and covered by multi-coloured bougainvillea dripping from the roof and glowing in the last roaming rays of setting sun.

As Kenya's startling short dusk turned to night I hopped onto the veranda and banged at the door. A deep contralto voice called, 'Come in,' so I pushed and entered, expecting the usual upcountry farmhouse jumble of rough-built furniture, sagging armchairs and ancient sagging book-laden shelves. Instead, I saw an amazing elegance of glossy dark-wood furniture, comfortable chintzy settles surrounded by display cabinets and shelving filled with shining silver cockerels, bulls and prancing horses along with dainty figurines and porcelain I recognised as Dresden and Limoges.

Beneath a large chandelier in the room centre stood a slender young woman, framed in a theatrical cone of soft light and holding a glowing cigarillo – one of those expensive long brown things with pungent smoke and a sense of drama. Wearing a long white dress of material so sheer her slim figure showed through in vague outline, she stepped forward two paces and stopped; head tilted, nostrils flared, haughty dark eyes looking down a long nose. She snapped, 'Who the hell are you?'

Completely stunned I stared, for a moment certain I had somehow stepped out of Africa and into an old movie, a feeling intensified by the hint of America in her voice. I tried to reply but my throat gummed up so she snapped 'Answer me, damn it. Who the hell are you?'

She came forward again, gown swirling. Out of the spotlight, her face changed from young and pretty to quite old and heavily made up and – thank God – her figure faded from view. I managed to get my throat working and stuttered, 'Your local policeman.'

'Nonsense,' she said. 'You're too young.'

Then in a complete change of mood she relaxed and said, 'Would you care to stay for dinner? We have fish tonight and I haven't had a young man here for months.'

'No,' I said, 'No. It's not possible. I'm on duty. And I've been away five days and must get back to my station.'

'Have a drink then.'

'No time. I only dropped in to see if all is well. Do you have any problems?'

She became haughty again and snapped, 'No; none at all. Go if you must. I don't care a fig whether you stay or leave.' She stepped back under the chandelier and became again young and beautiful. I stumbled backwards from the house and ran to my Land Rover. With a wide grin my driver said,' I see you have met the Memsahib Mericani...'

'Shut up and get me back to Pencil Slats.'

Next morning a runner arrived with an imperious note on scented paper. "Dinner tonight at eight. Black jacket and white tie. Alice de Courcey."

Is the woman mad? I returned an apology, "No jacket, no white tie and away in forest on night ambush". In a fit of foolish good manners I added, "Some other time perhaps."

That night after bumping into an armed gang I spent a week, tracking through the mountainous forest. My askaris, employing great skill and energy, trapped and eliminated three nasty specimens. Within a few hours of my return to Pencil Slats another note arrived. "Dinner tonight at eight. Dress optional. Alice de Courcey.

This one ended, 'Please come.' In a surge of sympathy for the poor woman, all alone in her farmhouse, I replied, 'Not tonight. I'll come tomorrow at eight.' I didn't bother to say I'd been living rough for seven days; she probably had a spy in my camp and knew already.

Giving my driver instructions to return at eleven I trotted onto her veranda, ducking a trail of bougainvillea. She went through the same act as before; the contralto instruction to enter, the chandelier pose in a semi see-through gown – light blue this time – the dramatic cigarillo and the stepping forward with a snapped question, 'Do you like eating kanga?'

Again, taken aback at her abrupt welcome I said, 'Sure. Yes. I don't mind.'

'Just as well,' she said, 'Because that's what we have tonight. What's your name?'

I told her and she said, 'I am Mrs Alice de Courcey and you may address me as Alice.'

'Thank you,' I said and stood waiting for my next instruction.

Head tipped head back she aimed her imperious nose at me in a haughty stare, all Gloria Swanson ready for the camera. 'Come on then. Dinner is ready. Take my arm.' In a stately glide she led me to a dining room decorated with more expensive silver porcelain and gleaming dark-wood furniture. A succession of well-trained servants in starched white robes served a perfect dinner of soup, kanga and a dessert the like of which I had never experienced. I usually found guinea fowl tough and dry but her cook had some way of softening the muscular meat to a melting softness and flavour. 'You have a great cook,' I said.

'Not great to begin with,' she said in her deep voice. 'I taught him everything he knows and now he's a chef, not a cook.'

Until then she had hardly spoken, concentrating on eating, drinking and drinking and drinking. She went through two bottles of wine before the kanga course ended and turned to sherry with her cheese and coffee. The drink seemed to have no effect until she observed, 'You don't drink much.'

This seemed to start a motor in her mind because her voice dropped an octave and her eyes took on a glaze. She said, 'Oh for the early days here when men were proper drinkers, proper lovers and real characters. And we women matched them all the way.'

She sighed and closed her eyes. 'How thrilling were the thirties when first I came to Kenya with my husband. He had so much money we could do what we liked and we did, darling, we did.'

From that moment on she never again said my name, calling me always 'darling'. At the time I supposed that meant acceptance, although I later recognised it as the first stage of seduction.

With closed eyes she continued, 'That first visit seemed like heaven and changed my life absolutely. I loved safari in the bush, sleeping rough in those awful tents and watching the men shoot those poor animals. They were all so strong and virile – the men, not the animals – and such wonderful lovers. I couldn't get enough of them. After my husband died in Texas I collected his fortune and hurried straight back to buy this place and build my own heaven.'

She raised her arms and stretched, shoulders back, chest out. Her eyes shot open and flashed me a hot glance, full of meaning. Alarmed, I jumped up and squeaked, 'Thanks for a wonderful evening. I must go.'

Her eyes glazed over again and I saw the wine and sherry take command. She stood and swayed for a moment before taking my arm and leading me to the main room to peck my cheek before pushing me towards the door. 'Nighty-night darling. Sweet dreams. Come again.'

I turned to say goodbye and she had taken up position under her chandelier and became, again, a young woman, her whole stunning figure in full display through the filmy material. I must say she looked damned attractive.

Next morning, I took half a dozen prisoners down to court in Gilgil. Returning four days later I found another note summoning me to dinner that night so, dressed in my best starched uniform, skipped onto Alice's veranda at dusk to be summoned inside for a display of almost transparent yellow chiffon sweeping from shoulder to floor. Transfixed, I stared. She allowed the show for several seconds breaking the spell by growling, 'Why do you always come for dinner in uniform?'

'It's all I have.'

She shrugged, floated forward, took my arm and led me to another wonderful dinner,. We went through the same charade as before, eating in almost silence until she felt oiled enough to move to a large settee in the front room and resume her history. 'I used to be a ballet dancer. Trained in New York and met my husband while touring Texas. He fell for me on sight during Swan Lake' She hiccupped and giggled. 'I thought him an ugly old devil but found his money really-really attractive. We married a month after meeting and I've been rich ever since.'

Leaping up she said, 'Look at how I've kept myself in dancing trim.' She threw her arms high and swept into a twirl, her skirt swirling high to reveal tight muscular legs. In sudden excitement she cried, 'Come on. Let's dance,' and rushed over to an old wind-up gramophone, shuffled through a pile of records and put on a gentle dance tune. 'Hold me, darling,' she whispered. 'Hold me and dance.'

Oh God, I didn't know what to do. There I am in full police uniform, backing away from this crazy half-dressed woman wondering how to get out of the place. In a flash she grabbed me into a really interesting embrace. I couldn't help relaxing against her and moving to the same rhythm. I must admit I found it pleasurable – six months or so alone in the bush changes some of your perspectives, including, in this case, age difference.

I managed to escape unscathed around midnight when she slipped a damp kiss onto my cheek and whispered some drunken mumble I didn't catch. Called away on a three week patrol I returned, exhausted, to find a note demanding I attend dinner next day and come properly dressed. A parcel on my side table contained four shirts and two pairs of trousers. Sitting on my hard bed I agonised; should I go or not? Staring at my dirt floor and mud walled living quarters helped my decision. Why shouldn't I take some of the luxury on offer? At the very least I could thank her for the shirts and trousers. So – feeling fully justified – I presented myself on her veranda dressed in perfectly ironed and pressed blue shirt and trousers.

This time Alice opened the door before I touched the handle. She stood framed by light wearing a short filmy dress. 'Hullo, darling,' she said. 'I'm dressed twenties style tonight. Do you like it?'

Like it? She looked fantastic. Curiously bewitched I stood and stared, unable to break the spell she cast and discovered that after my six months in the bush older women start to look remarkably young. 'Don't just gawp,' she growled. 'Come in. I have much to tell you.' There followed our usual routine, dinner, drink, drink and drink then talk, talk and talk, though in my case listen, listen and listen.

It seems true that when you spend regular time with someone you become more and more like them and this set our pattern for the next several months during which she slowly changed the rules in a way so subtle I did not at first notice. I found myself drinking more and becoming quite entangled in her tales, her food and her increasingly deep stories.

'My first husband – oh what a cruel man, just like my father,' she groaned, brushing away tears. 'Both beasts; absolute beasts. So, when I found freedom here with the lovely bronzed young farmers and hunters I felt I'd found paradise. You've probably heard of the Happy Valley crowd and that was us. We gathered for all sorts of naughty parties that went on for days and nights, all swapping partners and drinking and dancing and playing wicked and quite sinful games – oh darling, such hilarity; such happiness.'

At first it sounded light-hearted fun but as I began to know her better a darker tone emerged, partly I think because I managed to resist her increasingly obvious advances. One night she wore so little she could have been nude and I left early. 'Why darling? Why not stay the night and keep me company?'

'I have to stand to with my men at dawn.'

With a deep and dirty chuckle, she growled, 'I'll help you stand to at dawn, darling.'

I backed out the door followed by her gurgling laugh. For a week I ignored an invitation a day but finally, drawn back to this strange woman, I surrendered and returned to find her in a mood so deep and depressed I feared for her sanity. In the fading light of sunset, she took me outside to a well-tended plot under a jacaranda tree. Pointing, she said, "I'll die soon and be buried here." After a superb but silent dinner we went to the lounge and sat in deep soft chairs by the fire sipping large glasses of brandy. Eventually very drunk, she wept and whispered, 'I'll never be able to live down some of the awful things I've done. My trouble is I fall in love too easily.' Leaning over she pulled a tiny pistol from a drawer

'I fell for a beautiful man, a hunter and gambler, a womanizer and rake but reformed when he met me, or so he said. I adored him and when he asked me to marry him in Paris I thought I'd entered heaven. Three days before our wedding he said he planned to go to India with another woman and jilted me. I insisted on lunch before seeing him off at Gare du Nord. On the way I bought this small pistol and before boarding I gave him a great hug and shot him through the chest. He didn't die and the French charged me with attempted murder but my clever lawyer argued crime of passion and got me off.'

She stared at the fire then at me in a hard direct gaze. With a stab of fear, I kept my eye firmly on the pistol ready to dive if it waved in my direction. Instead, in an abrupt mood switch she kicked her legs in the air and bellowed, 'The silly bastard deserved it but still married me two years later.' She tossed the gun across the room. I caught it checked to find a fully loaded Colt 38 with delicate pearl inlay handle, the perfect handbag gun. Opening the chamber, I tipped six bullets into my pocket with the gun.

Lifting her glass, she tipped a full measure of brandy down her throat. It must have been a big hit because she almost passed out, head rolling, body slumping. With great effort she regained control and turned large wet pleading eyes on me and whispered, 'It's easy for you. I'm falling in love and you're not." She rolled a great tear out of one eye and sobbed in a quite remarkable display of acting, given her condition. "Please stay with me.'

I admit that for a moment I found it difficult not to be seduced. Here I am inhibitions badly dented by a fair flood of alcohol, with a quite beautiful woman offering everything and doing her utmost to ensnare and pull me in. She curled herself up on the sofa and with a low giggle, murmured,

'You're quite safe. You took the bullets out of the gun.'

"Did you plan to shoot me if I said no?"

"Possibly. I hadn't made up my mind."

Another grip of fear passed through me. Is this woman mad? I decided to get out but before I could move she said, 'I fell in love with Lord Errol then hated him when he left me for another woman. Someone shot him that night on the Ngong road. They suspected me of the murder and questioned me for hours. Very exhausting.'

Taking this as one of her over-dramatic stories, I chuckled and said, 'Did you shoot him?'

She jerked upright. Her black eyes turned to sharp slits and stabbed me with a glare that cut deep into my heart.

She snarled, 'Do you think I'm stupid enough to answer that question? You police all try to trick me into confessing. I don't want you here ever again. Get out. Get out now and never come back.'

I jumped up and hurried out, tossing the pistol at her jacaranda tree as I went. Her mood must have changed immediately because within hours I received pleading letters to return. Instead, within weeks I arranged a posting to Mandera in the north-eastern desert bordering Somalia and Ethiopia. Here I spent two hard years of searing heat and danger from armed Somali cattle rustlers and shifta before transferring to the Hong Long police from which I retired thirty years later.

One pleasant evening at a Colonial Police reunion in London, several of us sat round telling stories of derring-do in odd corners of the old Empire, I decided to avoid the blood and thunder reminiscences with a gentler tale of the character who continues to intrigue my memory and told them about Alice. When my story ended, one grey and grizzled ex-officer laughed and said, 'Dear old fake Alice. She tried the same trick on half a dozen of us including me. She faked that whole story by taking on the character of Alice de Janzé one of the Happy Valley crowd from the 20s and 30s. The real Alice came from Chicago. Fake Alice came from Reading. She'd never trained in ballet. She started dancing in seaside shows and toured the American burlesque theatres. It's true she married a rich old fool in America. When he died on safari in Kenya she took all his money and set up the house you saw and became fascinated by Alice de Janzé. Real Alice killed herself ten years before you met fake Alice who did the whole story rather well and in the end probably believed it all herself.'

'How do you know?'

'I investigated her death. Just like the real Alice ten years before, fake Alice died in a bedroom filled with flowers. She used that small pistol you threw away. Alice de Janzé used exactly the same gun, so fake Alice acted her whole story almost precisely.'

'I didn't know she died. I'm sorry to hear it. But at least she went as she wished.'

For several days after the reunion this final sad story would not go away. Then one night, in the early light of dawn I woke from a dream of dinner with Alice. This happened often but this time I felt she hovered nearby. I needed to speak so whispered the truth, 'Throughout life there are people I meet and never think of again. But Alice, I think of you always.'

Hindsight

I hate these literary parties and all who attend.

I'm standing in a corner sipping wine and hating the usual crowd of no-hopers, hangers-on, failed writers, crafty-eyed agents and self-important publishers.

But this is not a book launch.

It is a film launch.

Some ghastly writer wrote a ghastly blockbuster that is now a ghastly film.

I cast my eye over the crowd, so tightly packed they cannot move properly, instead shifting in a slow whirlpool of shouting, laughing, flirting and deal-doing, the men hoping to make money, the girls hoping to make it with the men.

I see my agent forcing her way through the door, eyes speed-scanning the room. I've seen her use this technique many times. Arrive late, pick a target, home in and fire off a barrage of marketing-speak.

I wave.

She pretends not to see me.

Can't blame her. I'm several months behind with my current effort and she probably knows it will be several notches worse than my last.

Most authors start at the bottom and if lucky hit it with number eight or ten.

I did it the other way. My first book, a runaway worldwide success, shot off all the charts and made plenty of money.

I became a big name.

The next ten books I wrote showed the true depth of my talent. They slid down the scale one by one and number twelve, is, when finished, likely to plop off the end.

Will I ever be published again?

I hope Ghastly Author's fluky first is the best he can do. With luck he'll follow my downward trajectory and disappear.

I sigh with pleasure at the thought.

From across the room, a young woman catches my eye.

I send back a subtle response.

She drifts on the tide towards me.

This one is so different to most in this party who all appear to be manufactured in the same blonde-and-pretty moulds used by the film industry.

She's short and almost dumpy. She wears spectacles and ordinary clothes and her face, smiling a greeting, is pleasant, intelligent and un-fussed by several millimetres' of makeup.

'Are you alone?' she asks.

'Except for this friendly wine glass.'

She chuckles. A pleasant, attractive gurgle.

'What about you?' I say.

'I came in with him,' she says, pointing at a tall skinny man with sandy hair and old-fashioned round glasses.

'That guy surrounded by all those women? What's the attraction?'

'Money. He's a multi-billionaire. He financed the film.'

'Is he your boss?'

'No. He's my lover.'

'Then why are you bothering with me?'

'Because he's a prat.'

Now I laugh.

'I've never met a billionaire prat. Come to think of it, I've never met a billionaire.'

We giggle and chat about nothing in particular and I find her great fun.

'I like you,' she says. 'You are amazingly normal. Take me out of here to somewhere quiet where we can be friends and perhaps make love.'

This casual and direct approach is quite normal for these functions.

I think for a moment and decide. 'No. Best not to. I have work to do after I leave. It can't wait.'

She shrugs and pouts.

'Next time perhaps?'

'Perhaps.'

We shake hands and I go home to my silent flat and my typewriter with its half-finished page and know, with perfect hindsight, that I should have taken up her offer.

Two years later I walk in tropical pre-dawn glow along the cool sands of a Caribbean beach.

Amazingly, book number twelve is a fantastic success and I am right back to the top of the tree, living the dream and spending the money.

Other things are changed. The ghastly film is rather good after all and Ghastly Author a fine fellow, now a close friend.

Sand squidges under my bare soles and forces itself between my toes, tickly and damp.

Some way ahead a woman walks towards me, probably feeling the same cool early morning pleasures. Wearing large pink sunglasses, a wide-brim floppy hat, a bright blouse and multi-stripe sarong, she is a splash of colour on the yellow beach.

We come closer and she waves.

I wave back.

'Hullo again,' she calls.

Again? Do I know her?

She whips off her hat.

My god. The multi-billionaire's concubine. She of the direct approach.

Dropping her hat, she hugs me.

Her attractive chuckle gurgles in my ear.

She says, 'Who'd expect it? What are you doing here?'

'Relaxing after two hard years. What about you?'

'Same as before, but this time with a millionaire. Not so much money, but a better class of prat.'

I say, 'Come one, I'll buy you breakfast at the beach cafe.'

I turn and we wander together.

At some point she takes hold of my hand.

'I read your book,' she says. 'Wonderful.'

'Glad you liked it. Someone is discussing a film.'

She eats fried eggs with a fork. Yolk dribbles down her chin. I fight hard against becoming entranced.

'Tell me about your millionaire.'

She waves her fork. Yellow spots scatter on the white tablecloth.

'As I said, he's a prat. He'll never leave his wife. Why don't you and I run away and get married?'

I laugh and say, 'You need millionaires and billionaires, not a poor hack like me. I'll never be that rich.'

'No, but you're fun. And you're interesting. And money doesn't matter.'

How could I believe her? This woman collects men with oodles of cash, currencies, private planes and mansions.

'In any case,' she said, 'you'll make plenty when your book goes to film. Come on. Let's run for it. Right now. I'm sick of living on that yacht. The damned thing never stays still.'

It worries me that I can't see her eyes behind those dark glasses.

I wipe her chin and the table with a napkin.

I give her hand a pat and say, 'Not possible.'

'Damn. I know what it is. You're married and won't leave her.'

I stand and walk away leaving her to sit there, still eating the egg.

Back at my lonely beach bungalow I watch the sun rise and wish I had more courage.

In hindsight I should have jumped up and run away to a new life with someone I could surely love.

Another two years later I bump into her in a Hollywood street.

'Oh, not you again,' she says with that wonderful chuckle.

'What on earth are you doing here?' I ask.

'I'm back with my skinny billionaire prat. He financed your film and we came for the Oscars. I felt so proud when you went up for the Best Writer Award. Buy me a drink and I'll propose to you again.'

I did and she did.

We elope and marry in Monaco.

'No yacht?' she laughs. 'I thought everyone in Monaco had a yacht.'

'I'll buy one.'

'No, don't. Those days are over. I love you as you are. Not quite a millionaire is quite enough.'

But it wasn't.

Four years later a young attractive billionaire catches her attention and she moves out as fast as she can.

'I may be older than him,' she says, 'but his bank balance is bigger than yours and he's better looking.'

After our divorce I sit in my luxury high-rise apartment and wonder if I am missing her.

I decide that, in hindsight, I should never have become involved.

On the other hand, with hindsight being such an exact science, I did find her great fun.

And so, I guess, do her millionaires and billionaires. Or why would they bother?

I whistle for my little white dog.

She scampers across and skips onto my lap for a cuddle.

I tickle her ear and whisper, 'Damn hindsight, little girl. The present is so much better. Don't you think?'

Four Stages of Christmas

Lubbecke, West Germany, December 1946

During those few weeks before Christmas a crushed people rise, determined to enjoy this first properly celebrated Festive Season since 1938. Although only eleven, the small English boy feels the melding of prehistoric Nordic rites and ancient Middle Eastern mysticism that form the enforced and gluttonous jollity of a properly run Teutonic Christmas.

Where does all this food come from? And all this drink? Beer, schnapps, wine and pear brandy by the carboy. And heavy dark-green fir trees, laden with a brilliance of coloured lights and tinsel and candles.

Invited to Festive celebrations by so many friendly German families and walking home stuffed with food and carrying presents, guiding his tipsy parents through crisp sparkling snow, he cannot understand six years terrible slaughter between such happy people. Instead of wrecking a continent, why didn't they just meet once a year for a big party?

Malindi, Kenya Coast, December 1957

Wondering if life anywhere else could be better than in this stunning Colony, the young man relaxes at a beach hotel with a circle of new friends brought together by Christmas. Across silver sand and sparkling surf, he watches triangular dhow sails skim the horizon, white and pure against the gentle blue sea.

He hears the mellow lunch gong chime. Indolent from a morning of surfing and flirting in hot East African sun, the group stirs. Strong tanned boys and delicious golden girls in bright bikinis stand, stretch and pad barefoot towards the dining room. He follows.

Who should I choose to sit by? The slim blond with the smallest bikini? Or the chunky red head with a great smile and lots of character? Or should I wait for evening and the dinky little receptionist who'd promised much with her eyes and one fluttering touch as he passed by?

Someone newly out from England says, 'How funny to have Christmas in the sun.'

Someone else says, 'Why? What about the first Christmas?'

An English Village, December 1967

Hurrying halfway round the world, the international businessman reaches home in time for the first Christmas party. Though exhausted from travel and burdened by mid-life problems – demanding job; demanding mortgage;

demanding children; demanding first wife – he determines to enjoy the evening.

It turns out to be the usual slow-dancing-in-a-darkened-room affair. Entwined couples glued together by dreamy music and the tantalising prospect of a little light adultery. Then home to the usual late-night recriminations.

An English Country Town, Early New Millennium

Christmas dinner done, the elderly gentleman sits in warm candle-lit quiet and studies his group of friends. Some slumped and dozing in soft chairs. Others murmuring tales of grandchildren and operations and aches and pains.

His mind wanders across the violent early years, passes through the difficult middle years and blesses good fortune for arriving safe, sound and healthy in these twilight years.

Across the room his calm and gracious second wife sits framed by candle-glow. She smiles and thirty years of delicately nurtured love passes between them.

Dinner at Sally's

Scouting for film locations in a run-down area just East of the City of London, I spied a small restaurant called "Dinner at Sally's". The menu on the door offered Coq-au-Vin, spelt in capitals C-O-C-K O V-A-N.

I stepped in. Several customers chumping through a large pile of well-gravied chicken looked up.

A woman – probably late thirties – sat by the till, elbows on the counter, blowing clouds of smoke at the ceiling.

'Do you have a table for one?' I asked.

'Come in, Darling,' she called in a loud, almost Cockney squeal, frizzy blonde hair swaying as though corn in a breeze. She waved a badly manicured hand. Words gushed from lips painted bright red.

'Sit down Sweetie and choose your din-dins.'

I laughed. 'I'll try the special please. But why do you spell it like that?'

'It's French, you know,' she bellowed. 'None of the people around here can read that Frog language, so I English-ised it. I wanted to call it Cock-In-A -Van, but Willie said that may be rude.'

I chose a table and sat. Hopping from her stool she swayed over on high heels, to lean on my shoulder and whisper, 'Don't see many posh young gentleman this part of London? What you looking for? Cheap diamonds? Cheap clothes? Cheap girls? We got plenty of all three.'

'Just a good lunch will do, thanks.'

She wiggled away, struggling to balance on the heels, struggling to clamber back on the stool in a bright flowered dress so tight, I feared it may split at the seams.

I ate an excellent lunch with treacle tart and custard for pudding and a cup of first-class coffee.

'Great food,' I said as I paid.

'Of course, my Lovely. That's why my customers keep coming back. Some of them are a bit odd, but they like my food and I love them all.'

She blew me a kiss. 'Come back soon, my Precious.'

Over the next few days, I found three likely locations and to celebrate returned for dinner at Sally's. 'I'll have the same again if it's available.'

'Don't worry,' she said with a lewd grin. 'Cock's always available here.'

I laughed and ate my dinner. As I paid, she again asked, 'What you doing here Duckie?'

'Some other time,' I said.

A few days later, while again tackling a huge plate of chicken, an elderly man, tired lined face, stained brown suit; slid into the seat opposite and murmured in a cultured accent, 'The white swallows are flying south over Serbia.'

Not sure how to respond, I said, 'Are they?'

He stamped a foot and glared. 'That's not today's password, you fool. You're supposed to say, "And the Bulgarian hunters are waiting to shoot them for supper."'

I managed not to laugh.

'Why do I have to say that?'

'I just told you. It's your half of the bloody password.'

He reached into his pocket and handed me a tightly rolled hand-made cigarette.

'Pass this on to Q. Soon as you can. Give it to no one else. Only Q. For his eyes only.'

He tapped the side of his nose, slid off the seat and slouched out through the door.

'Who on earth is he Sally?'

'He comes in often. He says he used to be a Russian spy. Or perhaps a German. He can't remember. He's harmless and has been watching and trailing you for a couple of weeks.'

'Why?'

'Cos you won't tell us why you're here my little Bundle of Sugar. That makes you a man of mystery. So he probably thinks you're a spy too. He's done the same with other people.'

I began to know Sally's, mostly, eccentric customers. The retired wrestler, a huge man, aged around sixty, no longer working, but still training. 'Trying to get back into the circuit,' he said. 'Bastards banned me for over-acting.'

And Jenny. A sweet, untidy young thing who touched my leg under the table and suggested a short time.

'Thank you, but no. I don't have time.'

'Not even a short time?'

'Not even a short time, I'm afraid.'

'She's not really on the game,' Sally told me. 'Poor Jenny wants to give it a go to spite her Mother, our local religious fanatic. Mummy won't let her do anything. Not get a job, a boyfriend, no dancing, no music at home, no sport. She's only allowed to stand on the pavement with religious posters on a stick and she sees the street girls at it and wants to have a go. But you're the only one she's dared ask, because you look like a nice man and you're sure to refuse.'

My work in East London finished, I followed other jobs to find locations for other producers. When filming started on East End Boy I went back to see how they were getting on and drifted round the corner to Sally's for dinner to find her café a charred wreck; completely burned down. Utterly destroyed.

Staring in shock I felt a tap on my shoulder and turned to find the old spy staring up at me.

'Did you pass it on to Q?' he asked.

'Of course. I always do what the Service requires.'

'Good man. If you're looking for Sally, she's gone. One night the building blew up and burned down. We never saw her again. The police searched in case she went with the building and said she must have been vaporised in the explosion. We held a wake, but it wasn't much fun.'

'Sad,' I said.

'Very,' he said. 'A lovely woman. Fond of you. Always spoke highly. When you see Q, give him my regards.'

Three years later in Paris, I saw a smart very pretty young woman coming along the crowded Champs Elysée elegantly balanced on stiletto heels. She looked familiar. As she passed, I tried a quiet, experimental, 'Sally?'

She stopped and smiled. In a refined accent she said, 'I recognised you and hoped you would not know me. Typical spy. I hope you are well.'

'I'm fine thanks but look at you. Not the East End Sally at all. We all thought you were dead.'

'Good. That's what I want.'

'What happened?'

She didn't smile. She grinned. A sort of superior twist of the lips and a cunning glint in the eyes.

'I started on the stage, Darling. Terrible life. All work, wandering hands and no money. So when I realised, that a tiny electric spark and a whiff of escaping gas could work wonders on my bank balance, I entered the catering profession, became Sally, and have been doing very well ever since. In London as Sally. Of course I'm not Sally in here

Paris. Nor have I been in Milan, in Berlin, Geneva or Stockholm. Local names work so much better. I won't invite you to lunch at my new place, in case you spill the gaff, so to speak. And we will never meet again, by accident or design, if you don't mind.'

With a pouted kiss, and a wiggle of her finely manicured fingers she turned away to go on down the Champs. This time a quite beautiful woman. Well worth watching until she disappeared in the swirling throng.

I've thought of her a great deal after this encounter and discussed an idea with my producer friend.

I found the locations.

He wrote the script.

The film Dinner at Sally's comes out in June.

Being a Ghost is a Lonely Thing

'What a pleasure to meet you.

I've been wandering around this castle for almost a thousand years and you're the first ghost I've met.

When did you come?

Only three hundred years ago?

Your Scots husband died in battle with the English?

I died fighting the Normans near Hastings.

No. Being Scottish, you wouldn't have heard of the place.

Oh, you had your head cut off. How terrible. They did that sort of thing in those days.

How did I die? Yes, that bit of wood sticking out of my left eye is an arrow. That's what killed me, and it's been a nuisance ever since.

You thought I wore it as a decoration? No. I wouldn't carry it around to show off. I promise; it's an arrow.

Of course, I can't get it out. If I could, I've have done so a thousand years ago.

Yes, it hurt for a few seconds. The same with your head, I suppose. By the way, could you please put your head back on? It's unnerving talking to you with your eyes looking at me from under your arm. Especially when I have to lipread.

Yes, I'm sure children find it funny and interesting, but it probably frightens their poor parents.

And please stop floating around the room With only one eye it's difficult for me to follow your movement and it is good manners to bring your head down from the ceiling and talk to me face to face.

Of course you can hold it up. Much better than under your arm. No, not too high. A bit lower, please. That's better. It looks almost normal and easier for me to see.

Yes, I know I only have one eye. Didn't you hear me tell you that?

Why can't I pull it out? Because it doesn't really exist, I can't get hold of it properly. No, I don't think you can help. Thanks for asking, though.

Yes, I agree. Haunting is a lonely task. But I quite enjoy making children laugh by going in and out through these thick stone walls, although oddly, it frightens the parents.

No really. The parents quiver and cry.

I wish you wouldn't ask what it is like have an arrow in my eye. Do I discuss your stupid head floating about up there? Please bring it under control and get it down from the ceiling.

Well, I'm sure it's a very good joke for children, but I find it unnerving. Which bit of the castle do you haunt?

Good. A long way from here. Why don't you go back there now?

No, I did enjoy meeting you. And yes, I will miss you. Please don't cry. I didn't mean to upset you.

Thanks anyway, but I'd prefer not to have a kiss.

Yes, you too. By the way, if you see someone who knows about bad eyes, please send them to see me.

The Dutchman

London June 1945

I marched into the office and saluted in my usual incompetent fashion. The two Army Intelligence Officers sitting at the desk frowned. I didn't care. Saluting when undercover in France we did not do. I'd forgotten the finer points of waving my hand up to forehead and back down and didn't care.

'We're investigating a possible murder in your Resistance Group, Captain Mellows', said the Major. 'We'll ask questions and you answer with all detail.'

'No, sir,' I said. 'You sit and listen without interruption while I tell you the whole story.'

The two men looked at each other for a few seconds before the Colonel said, 'Very well. Sit down and get started.'

Normandy August 1944

On the edge of a forest clearing, with summer light fading to darkness, I spread my small group of young French and English Maquis into a defensive semicircle.

'Enemy Intelligence knows we're in the area,' I whispered. 'Listen hard, keep watch as best you can and do not shoot unless in immediate danger. If any Boche patrols come near, get down, keep quiet and let them go by. It's important we safely collect our visitor and move away from here.'

Absolute silence fell and I waited in the warm night air with my ten men and one late teenage girl. I knew they were as tense as me, listening for the light aircraft due about now and hoping it would arrive before the Germans.

After a few minutes I heard the murmur I recognised as a Lysander engine approaching. 'Torches on for the count of ten,' I hissed.

Twelve bright beams flashed into the sky. The engine noise turned towards us, faltered; turned to a cough and splutter; then complete silence. Heart in my mouth, hoping it had been turned off for a quiet glide-in landing, I waited for the swish of wings through air. Ten seconds passed and off went our torches.

Instead of a noiseless landing, the sound of an object smashing through branches filtered through the forest. I wasted no time. 'Up and away,' I ordered in a whisper loud enough to carry. 'Follow me.'

Before my group had formed up, I heard footsteps coming towards us; a gentle brushing sound of feet and legs pushing through bush and grass. We all dropped to firing position on the floor; guns aimed. The footsteps halted.

"Lights,' I whispered.

In the beams stood a tall man in peasant clothing, hands raised. Speaking English with a flowing Dutch accent, he said, 'Ah. Found you.'

'Password?' I snapped, then 'Codename?'

Both correct.

'Keep your hands up and come forward.'

'Do you want my real name?'

'No.'

I ordered one of my men to give a quick body search for weapons. He found nothing.

'You're not armed?'

'No. If the Germans catch and search me, I am a Dutch carpenter looking for work. London ordered me to remain clean until we rendezvous, when you will give me weapons from your arms store.'

I stood and shook his hand. 'Welcome. We'll stay tonight at the farm. We have a few weapons there. Tomorrow at first light we move to another operational area for an important task.'

'Where are we going?'

'You'll know when we get there.'

Next morning, I broke my group into pairs and singles, and gave them different travel routes towards the east, using a map to point out a small town. 'We meet here at Café Noir in the main square in two days. If you don't make it in time, make for this village, a day further on and go to the Pension des Artisans. The patron will direct you to our safe house. We'll be there for three days.' To our young woman I said, 'Better if you travel alone. Patrols or sentries will let you through with a smile.'

We set off on our separate journeys at hourly intervals. I paired with the Dutchman and we went last. Before leaving, Edouard, my wireless operator told London we were on our way to Code Point Four.

'We're going by bus and train,' I told the Dutchman. He said, 'I want you to know my real name and hometown.'

'Why?'

'If I am killed you can let my family know.'

'Very well.'

'I am Jan van Heeren from The Hague. Everyone knows us. My family will welcome you.'

Over two days my group straggled into CP4 except for Young Woman. We moved on to CP7 to discover from London that she had been caught and shot at a roadblock with the farmer carrying her in his farm cart. We also heard that our arsenal had been raided and the French Maquis guarding it arrested.

On the next leg of our journey, two of my men failed to turn up, including Edouard and his wireless. Unable to tell London where we were and suspicious, we harboured a traitor. All swore loyalty on their mother's lives. To keep watch on my remainders I broke my rule and we all travelled within my eyesight, using trains and buses.

Nearing our target, Lyon, I saw three more of my men taken from the crowd at train or bus stations. It seemed obvious that one of my remaining five must be the traitor. Near Lyon, we camped by the River Rhone and cooked some food.

I waited until dusk and ordered them all to leave their weapons and line up on the bank. 'One of you is a Nazi spy,' I said. 'Step forward and speak up now to be arrested and save yourself from being shot later.'

The Frenchmen looked at the Dutchmen. He smiled and stepped forward, pulling a light machine pistol from under his coat, aimed it at me and said, 'I am arresting you all. We have known for some time your target may be a senior official in Lyons but needed to be certain. I have a Wehrmacht platoon nearby to detain you. Stand still while I call them with my whistle. Anyone who moves I will shoot.'

Before I could speak Jean-Louis, right of the line, turned and, with a small pistol, shot Dutchman through the face. The traitor fell back into the river to be swept away by the ferocious Rhone current.

'I told you to leave your weapons.'

'Sorry, Captain,' said Jean-Louis. 'I thought you meant our army weapons.'

'Break camp and run,' I said. 'Take only your personal bags. Go now.'

'I made my way north and met up with our advancing Army and here I am now,' I said to the two officers.

'Nothing else to say?' asked the Major.

'No, Sir.'

"We know of your reputation, Captain. So please confirm that Jean-Louise murdered the Dutchman, not you?'

'Yes, Sir,' I lied. 'Jean-Louis shot the Dutchman. And threw him into the river, knowing he'd never survive that fast flow and awful currents.'

'Then I think we're done. Thank you Major.'

'Captain, Sir. I'm a Captain.'

'No. We just promoted you.

Berlin November 1948

As part of a delegation negotiating the Berlin Airlift, I met an East German diplomat who looked remarkably familiar, his face twisted by a serious bullet wound scar.

He bowed and said, 'My name is Johann von Herrengast.'

His German had retained a hint of the flowing Dutch.

'I think we met in Normandy during the war,' I said.

'I don't think so. I saw action only against Russia. Never did I go to France.'

'Yes, you did. Only then you were a Dutchman called Jan van Heeren.'

'My dear Colonel Mellows. You are mistaken.'

'No. You are van Heeren.'

He took my arm. 'May we speak privately Colonel.'

He guided me to a small private room and said, 'Listen Mellows. I used to be a Dutchman, but now I am a German from the Democratic Republic. I managed to get out of the river after you tried to illegally murder me, your prisoner of war. So, we make an arrangement. You keep quiet about me and I keep quiet about you. I am sure you know precisely what I mean.'

I turned and walked out. Three days later I left Berlin. At the Airport I read of a senior East German communist drowned in the River Havel near Spandau. The police found no suspicious circumstances and wrote the death off as accidental without an inquest.

Perhaps they did not bother to fully investigate the case of a communist agent. Or perhaps failed to notice he died by pressure on a nerve near the major artery carrying blood to the brain. This little-known trick we used in France during the war to kill informers.

Interesting to see it still worked.

Behind The Painted Smile

1915 - The First Picture

In late afternoon sun The Artist stands on his veranda watching the Mediterranean push small waves ashore, his mind working on various shades of shimmering blue.

His attention turns to a young woman walking barefoot along the beach, carrying tiny pink shoes in one hand, and a sun parasol in the other.

He squints to study better the softly swaying material of her purple and pink ankle-length skirt. She comes gracefully towards his gate, long toes flicking up white grains of sand.

She walks up the path between pale hibiscus, red roses and nodding green grasses.

His heart beats faster at this riot of colour and he fights an urge to rush to his studio and paint before the vision flees his mind.

The young woman waves.

At last he looks at her face; later described as elfin. A sweet smile, honey-coloured hair unfashionably long and almost perfect bone structure. Precisely what he has been seeking for months.

The Artist steps down to meet her.

'Hallo,' she says. 'I'm a journalist. I want to interview you.'

'Come in,' he says.

She writes for a prestigious Paris art magazine. Over coffee he pretends to answer her questions.

She stays the night and next morning, at dawn, agrees to be his Model and Muse.

1925 – The Second Picture

Walking just after dawn along the pebbled beach at Cagnes, The Artist watches early swimmers abandoning the chill water for warmth and the rising sun.

He studies them stumbling on the occasional sharp pebble, shoulders hunched, bodies twisting away from the pain. He watches them rub down hard and buff vigorously their heads, before stretching on pebbles or beach bed to soak up the bright sunlight.

The sketchpad in his mind works at furious speed, preparing images and colours to be painted before noon.

He watches a swimmer racing back to shore through a cloud of sparkling spray. She reaches the shallows and stands.

He sighs in delight at her beautifully constructed face. White skin shaped by perfect cheekbones below a wide brow. To his artist's eye her long shape – not over-muscled – fits precisely into the frame he would use to paint the picture he planned the moment he saw her rise from the sea.

Before she finishes towelling, he offers a café crème and croissant.

They sit together and chat across a spindly table on the promenade edge.

Recognising him, she says, 'I thought you had long hair.'

He rubs his scalp.

He says, 'My curls and I are parting company.'

She laughs.

After a second café crème and two more croissants, she agrees to be his Model and Muse.

1945 – The Third Picture

Bored and wondering how to get out of this dull gathering, of second-rate painters and dealers, The Artist sits on a hard sofa, his frustration at being trapped almost boiling over.

A very small young woman approaches and sits next to him.

'You don't look very happy, she says.'

'I've no reason to be.'

She giggles.

'But you have. I hear you sold your last painting for thirty million dollars. Is that right?"

'Probably. I never know. My agent will tell me.'

He turns and stares at this upstart, so tiny he feels a brisk breeze would blow her away.

With a sweet smile she offers a hand.

He takes it; afraid to press hard on fingers so delicate they could be a bundle of twigs encased in silken skin.

Looking into her large round eyes his artist's intuition senses deep and abiding avarice.

Her head looks almost too large for such a slight frame.

He finds sudden fascination in a slightly uneven face - broad forehead; those big eye sockets; that pointed chin and the short cut jet black hair worn as a hat - all combine in the perfect shape for one of his lopsided paintings.

'Come on,' he says. 'Let's not waste time here.'

They slip out and he takes her to supper.

Even before dessert she agrees to be his Model and Muse.

1975 – The Auction

The Auctioneer taps his gavel.

The murmur of intellectual conversation dies away.

The Auctioneer starts his pre-sale pitch.

'We have only three paintings for you today. Although painted twenty-five years apart they are always bought, sold and held as a trio, known as Behind The Painted Smile. According to The Late Artist's will, they must never be separated.

'The first picture, from 1915, entitled Girl In A Blue Dress is considered to be a sombre study of the end of marriage. The model – his wife and a famous writer– is painted with a carefully contrived half smile giving us a hint of their life of conflict. She sits, head tilted, drawing our gaze to those ruby lips and sad eyes.

'Only days later she abandoned The Artist. She fled, taking their baby son.

'We can only wonder that The Artist's early talent showed the depth of her distress with a few subtle hints and simple brushstrokes.

'The second picture, from 1925, entitled Girl From The Beach shows a young woman he met during his morning stroll. As an international swimmer, her stunning physique precisely fitted a series of planned paintings.

'She became his constant companion and lover for eight years, modelling many famous paintings, but disliked the way he destroyed her beauty during his Surrealist period. This picture is an example. Note the enormous bust and nose, neither of which she had. And one large blue eye set on her cheekbone, the other, painted green, staring from the centre of her forehead.

'Observe the thickly painted lips, that we see as a frustrated grimace or grin. The Artist shows her inner disquiet with astonishing skill.

'A year later she hanged herself from a tree in their garden. Although he had professed great love, The Artist showed no remorse and never spoke of her again.

‘The third picture, from 1945, entitled Girl On A Garden Chair is of an unknown woman The Artist came to hate. It is said that they met when she accosted him at a party and brazenly asked how much his latest painting sold for. He professed not to know, but spellbound by her tiny body, outsized eyes and almost heart shaped face, persuaded her to become his Model and Mistress.

‘He soon realised that her abiding passion – money – ruled her life and began to take over his. She sat only five times during their eight months together and took more than thirty paintings when she left, apparently filching from his chaotic store on a regular basis.

‘This final picture he painted of her cleverly demonstrates his utter dislike. He shows her face as an ugly triangle tipped at an angle that jars with the rest of a symmetrical portrait. In obvious insult he places her large round eyes as awkward almonds, one standing on end, the other laying across her left cheek.

‘And he paints her smile as a sudden V in two sardonic coils past her nose and cheekbones. Is he indicating, perhaps, the classic pencil-thin moustache of the conman?

‘The paintings this woman took have turned up at auction during various times since The Artist’s death. So we assume that the mysterious lady in question has become very rich.’

The Auctioneer gazes down, knowing his audience is poised and primed.

In two seconds he will hit them with the opening price.

A rear door opens.

A tiny woman slips through and takes the only remaining seat.

The Auctioneer has time to note her short-cut jet-black hair, large eyes under a broad forehead and oddly pointed chin.

He takes a deep breath.

'Our opening price is eighty million dollars.'

The tiny woman flicks up a finger and The Auction starts.

The Long Shadow

The long shadow of the prison watchtower traverses the yellow prison yard sand from wall to wall and dawn to dusk. For the ten years I've been here it has been my hour hand for every day I've been in this cell. I thank the harsh Texan sun that gives me this timepiece. Without it I would certainly have gone mad.

I remember arriving in this place mentally dead from the terrible year of arrest, trial and sentence, standing in the Governor's office for examination and interrogation.

A huge hard-eyed man leaning back in his chair, running eyes over me and wearing the large, brimmed Stetson that all these people use, indoors and out, he flicks through my file and says, 'So you're a Britisher hey? What are you doing in a Texican jail?'

'That's what I keep asking,' I say. 'I shouldn't be here at all.'

'Shouldn't be here at all,' he says, in a poor mimic of my English accent. 'I guess you didn't do it, hey, Buddy? I guess you didn't kill that guy.'

'If I had, no one would ever have known.'

'Let me tell you Pal, that my jail is full of innocent guys. Not one killed or raped anyone. Not one should be here. They say.'

He points at a page. 'This here says you're a doctor. What sort?'

‘I’m a psychiatrist.’

‘Just what we need here Doc, Baby. You may be of use.’

I stare at him, silent and resentful. He dismisses me to a dark and lonely cell in the bowels of the building. After two weeks he summons me.

‘Well Doc, he says, ‘I have a job for you.’

‘No.’ I say. ‘I’ll work for no one while I’m in here.’

A month goes by and he calls me in again. ‘Listen Doc, I got a dozen baddies in special security. They’re brutes I can’t control. I need your help to calm them down. You gotta do something to help me. You are a psychiatrist, right?’

‘I am. And I’ve dealt with and improved many such men. I’ll help you if you help me. I need a cell with a window and sunlight. I need a desk and chair. I need a bookshelf and all books I tell you to buy, plus paper and pens. And I need a comfortable bed with clean sheets every second day.’

‘Anything else?’

‘Yes. I need a proper consulting room to see these men one to one and all together for joint sessions with no guards. I’ll give you three months and see how it goes.’

‘Jeez, Doc. They’ll tear you apart. These guys are beasts.’

‘That’s my risk.’

'I'll fix it all, Pal.'

That is how I come to sit facing a semicircle of twelve murderers, rapists, paedophiles and vicious kidnappers. All huge men, muscled to the ears, covered in violent tattoos advertising their speciality.

Except for one; a small sweet-faced fellow with blond curly hair, soft eyes, a shy smile and no tattoos at all. He turns out to be the cruellest and most vicious of all. He frightens me more than all the others put together, but client confidentiality bars me from telling you why.

I ask each for identification and get only prison nicknames. Sweet-Face they call "Darling."

'Nothing naughty in it, Doc', he says in a soft voice. 'It's just the way I look.'

I ask the rapists to hold up their hands. I point at the largest and say, 'Why?'

'I needed a bit of sex Doc. Fast. And that seemed the best way to get it.'

'Yes,' I say. 'But there are other ways of understanding why. I've read up on your case. The way you rape indicates a personal crisis; perhaps something long hidden. From your childhood, for instance. That is what we should discover and discuss. Not the rape itself. Tell us more.'

He half closes his eyes and starts to explain. The others join in. And on it goes for three months. Conversations of disgusting crimes that ruin my sleep after every session. At each dawn, I lean on my windowsill watching the long tower shadow of my personal day, month and year drag from prison wall to prison wall for twelve hours and I hope to die soon.

I quickly realise that these terrible men are not boasting. They are telling me a truth never heard in court. They are confessing to a sympathetic stranger. I start meeting them individually. Together, face to face across a table, we analyse crimes and dig deep into reasons and reasoning.

It works. Before the three months end, I stand again in the Governor's office.

Leaning back in his chair, he squints at me and says, 'Hey Doc. You're a success. Those guys can't get enough of you. They're calm and want to cooperate. How the hell do you do it?'

'Trade secret,' I say. 'If I tell you, we'd have to swap. You take my cell and the sessions. I'll come in here and run the prison.'

He chuckles and says, 'Love your British sense of humour. You're doing something for me, so I'll do something for you. Here's the deal. Keep going for six months and I may be able to make your life more comfortable. Now get outa here and back to your classroom.'

Five months later I'm in his office again. I guess something must be happening because he stands to greet me.

'Well, Doc,' he says, tipping the brim of that ridiculous Stetson, 'I'm about to lose you. In a week you'll be gone. Free.'

Shock sweeps through my body. I shiver. I feel the room sway. 'How?' I ask.

'Didn't want to tell you before, Buddy, but six months ago your lawyers appealed. They won last week. After all this time, you're innocent. How does it feel?'

'The same. I've always been innocent. I told you when I came in here.'

His eyes turned shrewd.

'You can tell me Buddy. I'll never say a word. Honest. Did you kill that guy?'

'Of course not.'

But of course, I did. I could have injected him so no evidence would ever be found. He'd have died with a simple heart attack, no questions asked. But I deliberately left evidence to be caught, so she would know what I'd done. And how I'd done it. Revenge is sweet, especially when I gave him a lingering and painful death and her the mental agony of knowing she had caused it.

Before I stepped into my waiting limousine, I stood in the hot Texan sun, looking up at the high tower, knowing exactly where the long shadow would be at this time of day. And knowing it will be with me for ever.

'Are you comfortable, Sir?' asks my chauffeur.

'Very comfortable, thank you. Drive slowly so I can rest.'

I lean back with closed eyes and start planning how to deal with her. Not too much pain, I think. I want her gone fast. I know exactly what to use. And this time no one will ever know what happened.

The Catch

The Chief called me in.

'Ah, Wilkins, he said, 'I need you in Russia; St Petersburg.'

'You promised not to send me back after the last time.'

'Only a short trip, old boy. In and out. Not more than twenty-four hours.'

'What's the job? There must be a catch.'

'Yes. I need you to bring Kettering out. The catch is that he's disappeared. The Russkis broke his cover. He skipped the nest seconds before they bust the door down. Managed to flee with his secret pad. Probably swallowed the damn thing. We need him and the pad before it returns to daylight, so to speak. So, it must be a quick job. If all else fails and you can't bring him, just bring the pad.'

'Why not send Cottesloe or Kettering? They both speak Russian.'

'You're the only one with Finnish, old fellow. Damned difficult language. So, it must be you, I'm afraid. You're going in as a northern Finn.'

'If he's disappeared, how do I find him?'

The Chief pushed an operational directive across his desk. 'All there, old boy. We have someone to give you guidance. Follow these instructions to the letter until you find him. After that bring him home by whatever means you devise. Or at least, the pad. Good luck, old fellow.'

The following day a bricklayer stepped from the Helsinki train in St Petersburg's Finland Station, carrying his tools of trade and a contract to work on the big new police headquarters south of the city.

Stopped by two armed security men, I showed my work contract and speaking broken Russian in a thick North Finland accent, explained my reason for being in Russia. Of course, they could hardly understand a word, so let me pass with a rude joke about the stupid Fins.

I'd discovered in previous operations that being a humble bricklayer or car mechanic is always better than being a banker or businessman. With no class envy the lowest, most insignificant police or government official, feels enough kinship to assist a fellow struggler in the swamp. Or, at least, not to shove his head under too many times.

Following my instructions to the letter, I found the pavement café and sat at the third table from the left. I ordered black Russian coffee and one of their stickiest cakes, happy at remembering my favourite treats, enjoyed so often before being forced to flee those few years ago.

A young woman appeared from the passing throng and took seat at my table.

'You haven't changed,' she said.

'Nor have you,' I lied, to a face that had become thin, lined and weary, probably from the strain and apprehension endemic in the world of spying.

'You should have married me when we were lovers,' she said. 'We would have been happy.'

'Perhaps.'

Her lips twisted in a bitter smile.

'And now you need my help.'

'Yes. You are going to take me to our friend.'

'Impossible. He's dead. He ran from the flat and they shot him on the stairs.'

I controlled my shock with a wide smile and said, 'Well there's a catch. They told me he'd escaped, and you would arrange a meeting.'

I looked up and down the street.

'Don't worry,' she said. 'I'm alone and still working for you. And I have the security pad.'

'On you?'

'In me. He passed it to me and threw me out the door when he saw the goons arriving in big cars. I rushed up the stairs into a toilet and pushed it in the best hiding place I could think of. What do we do now?'

'Go to the Finnish embassy.'

'Why not the British?'

'Because my legend is that I'm a Finn. I'll never get past the Russian guards at the British gate. They can't stop me at the Finnish.'

'And what about me?'

'You are my Russian fiancée. We're going in to get your visa for Finland.'

'But I have no Russian exit visa.'

'You will in a couple of hours. Where can we go to make you look pregnant?'

'Why?'

'Because you need specialist treatment in Finland. And no one will examine you as we leave Russia.'

She laughed. 'A friend of mine runs a theatre shop. She'll help.'

We had no problem at the Finnish embassy. The Russian gate guards listened carefully and let us straight in without comment. A quick call to the British Embassy brought a young attaché carrying a suit, shirt and a tie for me, plus a diplomatic passport covering us both.

We were back at the Finland Station in an hour, my poor fiancée waddling as best she could and looking quite ill. Her theatrical friend had shown great expertise with stage makeup.

The diplomatic exit formalities worked without problem and four hours later we arrived in Helsinki. From there a private plane took us direct to London.

I walked into Chief's office eighteen hours after being given the order to bring back Kettering or the pad.

'Where is the woman?' he asked.

'In hospital having the pad recovered.'

I told him the whole story.'

'Well done Wilkins. You did well. But we have to do something with the woman. Diplomatic are already asking who she is and why is she here in Britain on false documents. If we're not careful we'll have to explain the whole pantomime you got us into and share our special intelligence and operative. I can't allow that to happen.'

He frowned, then began to chuckle. This is something the intelligence service had never seen. Always the stern boss; his face remained humourless and hard whatever the situation.

Even more surprising, he began to giggle

'I've got it,' he said. 'You'll have to marry her.'

'I can't.'

'Oh yes you can. After all, you got her pregnant in the first place. I told you there'd be a catch. Now we have what I call real catch.'

He leaned back in his chair and began to laugh without control. I think it must have been the first and only joke he ever made in his long dismal life.

So, I married the girl. As she said at that pavement café, I should have married her years ago when we were lovers in that magical city, St Petersburg, because we became a truly happy married couple. Retirement suited us both. The lines removed themselves from her face. She became the energetic and interesting woman I had known those years ago. We never spoke of our previous life of danger and intrigue.

And we never ever spoke of poor Kettering who finally brought us together in the strangest of ways.

The Amateur Dramatic Society

I checked my hair and makeup, adjusted the top of my dress to show a little more peek-a-boo, took a deep breath, and stepped into a noisy rehearsal room.

The twenty or so people standing in groups were too caught up with shrieking conversations, loud laughter and interrupting to notice me.

Confused and nervous, I stood wondering what to do, when a short, plump, energetic red-face man with a mass of ginger hair rushed forward to greet me. He grasped both my hands and shouted, 'Look everyone. Our new Member is here.'

He made not the tiniest dent on the bellowed exchange of whatever they were trying to tell each other, so looked up at me with adoring eyes and said, 'Wow. What beauty, what style. What's your name, honey?'

'Ann Wellington.'

'Ann Wellington,' he repeated, shaking his head. 'Not good enough.'

Hand to forehead and acting ultra-dramatic, he said, 'No; no; no. Not good enough for the stage, ducky. Sounds like a waterproof riding boot. Wait. I have it. We'll call you Elaine Delamere. You look Elaine Delamere, darling, so Elaine Delamere, you are.'

He clapped his hands, stamped his feet and jumped up and down, red face getting redder, until able to call above reduced hubbub, 'Look darlings. Here is our new member. Elaine Delamere. Isn't she delicious?'

A few turned, glancing with a nod, returning instantly to yelling at each other. 'Don't worry, sweetie,' he said. 'They'll soon get to know you.'

'What play are you doing?' I asked.

'It's a Coward comedy. Great fun.'

'Noel Coward?'

'No. Horace Coward.'

'Never heard of him,' I said, preparing to leave.

'He's me. I'm Horace Coward: playwright, actor and theatre manager.'

He bowed.

'At your service Ma'am. Although Horace Coward is only a stage name. I can be Horace Shakespeare, if you wish.'

'No. I'm quite happy with Horace Coward.'

'Good. Your beauty, charm and wit make you perfect for the part of Annabelle. I hope to God you can act.'

He picked up a heavy drumstick and walloped a pattern of noise on a large bass drum leaning against the wall.

Silence fell. 'I only bring this to shut them up,' he whispered, before dropping the drumstick, clapping his hands and calling, 'We're starting read-through. Positions at table please. Darling Elaine will read Annabelle.'

‘I thought I would be Annabelle,’ wailed a voice from the crowd. ‘No. You’re going to be Miaow The Cat, sweetheart. You Miaow better than anyone else.’

He turned to me and whispered, ‘Your first enemy, darling. Watch out for her claws. Can be lethal.’

I’d acted in my last school play five years ago, but must have done well as Annabelle, because everyone applauded. Except for Miaow The Cat, who literally sat on her hands, keeping them planted firmly under her sizeable buttocks. Horace showed enormous delight, rushing to me with a huge hug. ‘You have a wonderful future darling Elaine. We’ll make you a star.’

‘I’m Ann.’ I said.

‘No. You’re Elaine. You are Elaine Delamere for the rest of your life.’

That little red faced, red haired man knew his onions. What he called my natural gift for acting, made Annabelle the star of the show and so much money for the Society, at the end of an extended run, Horace, in a state of his usual excitement, cried, ‘We’ll turn you professional. Immediately. I’ll be your agent. We’ll travel the world. Hollywood, here we come.’

‘Don’t talk nonsense,’ I said. ‘I have a job and a boyfriend. I can’t go to Hollywood.’

But do you know, he turned out to be a brilliant agent. I cast off my boyfriend and married Horace.

He nursed me onto the London stage, took me into a few small films, until Hollywood called and cast me in an international blockbuster than made my career and our fortune.

'How did you manage it all?' I asked him twenty years after that first read through as Annabelle.

'Red hair,' he said. 'We gingers have a hard time. We're genes apart from normal hairs. You normals look down on gingers, forgetting how we stand out from the crowd. Trouble is I had to get it all done before turning grey. Look at me now. Lost in the crowd.'

When I went to the Palace - Buckingham, not the theatre - when they made me Dame Elaine, he had his hair gingered by the toppest of top theatrical makeup artist. 'Can't have any white showing,' he said.

And I must say, he looked short, plump, red-faced and with a mass of ginger hair, and just as energetic as the day we first met.

'You looked wonderful, darling,' I told him, looking at the photographs and television news.

'Yes,' he said. 'And what about handsome too.'

'I'm not sure I'd go that far, Horace my sweet.'

'Oh, go on. Just this once. You can do it, Dame Elaine. You know you can.'

'Very well,' I said and gave him a hug and a kiss. 'You do look handsome.'

'Ta,' he said. 'Shall I pour the tea or you?'

Beyond Belief

I walked that black November night along the track towards my house, sometimes feeling my way along the tall wet hedge. I could just make out the grim dark shadow of the building a hundred yards ahead, looming high towards heavy rainclouds.

Stopping to study the place as best I could and wondering why no lights shone from the windows, I trod across the noisy gravel and, feeling a certain amount of nameless fear, pushed at the door.

It opened.

I stepped into the silent hall and felt for the light switch. It must have been moved since last I came, so, navigating by fingertip along the wall, I trod with care into the main room, trying to avoid tripping or stumbling into furniture.

A door opened and the form of a woman stepped through, visible against what must have been candlelight from the kitchen.

'Is that you Mary?' I asked.

'It would be if I were here,' she said, 'but you killed me. You killed us all.'

'When? How? Where are the children?'

She stepped back and closed the door.

Using the palm of my hand on the wall, I started to follow. But the bricks and masonry began to fade from my touch, dissipating into a mist that drifted away on a light breeze, until the house no longer existed, leaving me standing in an empty field.

Rain began to fall. Completely confused, I sat down on wet grass and began to cry. The police found me next morning.

Three months later, the psychiatrist stared at me, legs crossed, pencil poised over his latest doodle.

'What you are telling me is beyond belief,' he said.

'I know. But it is the honest and absolute truth. It all happened as I told you.'

'I believe you. I've seen the police transcript. You gave me the same story in the same words. I went there a few weeks ago with a local historian and the farmer who owns the land, used his digger to excavate and found part of the original wall. The historian knew a house had been in that field during the sixteenth century but could find no record of what happened. The piece of wall we found showed evidence of a catastrophic fire. This led him to old church and parish records that pieced together a terrible story. You may not want to hear it.'

'Please tell me.'

'I'm not sure I should. You are still mentally fragile.'

'I need to know. Please set my mind at rest.'

'In the reign of Henry VIII, a rich farmer thought he discovered his wife in an adulterous affair. Whether correct or not, this sent him mad. He murdered his wife and six children and burnt the house down, to be convicted and hanged a month later. The village priest and parish beadle hushed the matter up, but you can read between the lines from different sources, including notes of his trial and hints in letters from villagers of the time.'

'So, what happened to me that night?'

'At dawn those six-hundred years ago, villagers found the farmer sitting on wet grass in the rain, weeping, just as you describe. So somehow your mental breakdown led you to that place to relive the whole incident from six-hundred years ago. Once there, an ancient feeling of guilt and desperation appeared to make you slip back in time to, perhaps, just after the tragedy. You may by then have been an ancient ghost but mixed with your modern self. This may be why you looked for non-existent lights to turn on. We have no other explanation.'

'But, as you said, that's beyond belief.'

'I agree. Absolutely beyond belief. But we wonder that, with treatment to clarify your modern mind using drugs, hypnosis and other techniques, your ancient ghost may return and tell us the whole story.'

‘Do I want that? Do I wish to really know I killed my whole family?’

‘Only you can decide. But you’ll probably gain one benefit. We may be able to clear a definite desire to kill we discovered in your deep subconscious. It may have been handed down through the centuries. You are a truly dangerous man.’

Chilled at hearing such a shattering diagnosis I did not hesitate.

‘Let’s get on with it then.’

Madame Sinskaya and Those Horrible Men

I'm sitting in the study moving money from Madame Sinskaya's account to my own, when the huge bulk of the lady herself moves along the corridor with the grace of a large sailing ship in a light breeze.

She tacks to port into the room, heaves-to alongside my desk, gathers the soft material of the bright purple tent she is wearing and settles onto chaise longue in the corner. For a moment I fear that her tall Edwardian hairstyle may topple, but, as with any well-built crow's nest, it sways, but remains just about in position.

She sighs and tears trickle down her cheeks.

I wonder why she is crying, so ask, 'Why are you crying?'

'Oh, darling little man, this is a sad day.'

I grit my teeth. Why does she always call me little man?

'Why is it a sad day?'

'Oh, my little man. It is the anniversary of the day those horrible men took over my beloved country.'

There you are. 'Little man,' again. Perhaps I should shoot or strangle her.

Instead I ask, 'What horrible men?'

She pats tears away with a tiny kerchief the same colour as her tent.

'Those horrible Bolshevik men Lenin and Trotsky. They overthrew that nice Mr Kerensky in a silly little coup they called a revolution then took our lovely Tsar from his estate and sent him to a place on the edge of Siberia.'

Tears flow again, but I remain still and silent. If I go across to comfort her she'll seize me in those wire-hawser arms, drag me into that great soft pillow of a chest and I'd be unable to escape or breathe.

She dabbed at her cheeks and set off once more on her story.

Feeling this may be a long haul I made myself comfortable.

'Until then, you understand, I had a wonderful life in St Petersburg. My husband the Grand Duke loved me but didn't mind me flirting with all those lovely young officers at parties and balls. We all dressed so grandly, the men in beautiful uniforms, all gold braid and buttons shining, we women in low cut dresses flowing and swirling as we danced. Of course, some ladies were a bit naughty with those dashing hussars, but nobody care. We lived such a charming life until those two horrible men took it away.'

More tears. Quite a flood this time.

'With our dear dead Tsar gone we started to fight back. Admiral Kolchak left his ships in the

Baltic and came down to set up an army in Siberia. How an Admiral could run an army made up of so many different groups including a Legion of Czechs, I don't know. The silly man should have stayed playing with his Baltic battleships. Instead he put together an army and a government called White Russians to fight those two horrible men and their Red Russians. My husband, the Grand Duke, insisted we flee St Petersburg and join Kolchak. I had a terrible journey. Would you believe that my husband only allowed me to take five trunks of clothes? Hardly enough to properly dress for dinner.'

Managing not to laugh, I murmured, 'Terrible.'

She said, 'Of course you, being so intelligent, can understand what humiliation I suffered. Only five trunks. And four were stolen while we travelled. How could I keep up socially with so little to wear? When we reached Siberia, Admiral Kolchak invited us to live with him on his armoured train. We were grateful, but I felt so dowdy when dining with him and his mistress, Anna Timiryova. She had left her husband, another Admiral, for Kolchak. Although of low birth and still without rank as Admiral Kolchak's fallen woman, she had such airs and graces because she had ten trunks and quite sneered at me with only one. I always feel this as the worst thing that happened to me during that ghastly civil war.'

Quite horrified at such selfishness, I said, 'But what about all those men shot or frozen to death?'

She waved a hand to dismiss such a silly intervention.

'The trouble with Kolchak is that he could not organise a government or an army. That horrible man Lenin ran a proper government and that other horrible man Trotsky became, without any military training, a brilliant general with his own armoured train. That ugly little devil Trotsky had no mistress, so he could concentrate on beating Kolchak, using brainpower as well as soldiers. He heard that the Czechs wanted to go home. To do this they had to find a way past his army, so Trotsky drew his men aside and gave them safe passage. Off they went and Kolchak knew he could no longer win. In February 1920 The Reds captured him and the awful Anna Timiryova. They shot the Admiral but let her go.'

I tried to interrupt to ask why, but she raised her voice and talked over me.

'General Kappel took command and retreated east towards China, our only hope of sanctuary. With Trotsky and his Reds close behind we came to the shore of Lake Baikal. Kappel had the choice to stand and fight or keep going across the frozen lake. He chose the lake and on that awful day a column of thirty thousand soldiers with their families and all their possessions set out in a gale blowing straight down from the arctic and a temperature of minus sixty degrees. Somewhere in the middle of the column a Guards Unit carried a fortune in the Tsar's gold that Kolchak had got his hands on.'

Madame Sinskaya began to weep again, this time in great heaving sobs, her face crumpled in distress at some awful overwhelming memory.

'You cannot believe the agonies of that terrible lake. People began to freeze and die as soon as we stepped on to the ice, whole families huddled together. I passed a young woman giving birth on a pile of greatcoats, surrounded by a group of gallant young officers facing outwards, their capes held high as a miserable barrier to save her from the wind. Around this time my husband disappeared and I saw him no more. I wanted to turn back, but my brave escort of fifteen Hussars would not allow it. So my husband stayed on that dreadful ice among a frozen tableau of bodies that remained until spring when the frozen corpses and all their possessions disappeared in five-thousand feet of water. My darling husband and the Tsar's gold sank with them.'

She continued sobbing and I must admit I came close to breaking down and sobbing with her.

But I hold on and say, 'But you got across the lake?'

She nods and blows her nose.

Recovering, she whispers, 'Yes. I got across the lake. Those of us who survived found shelter in a nearby town. A few days later that horrible man Trotsky and his Red Army crossed the lake and advance towards us, so those recovered enough able to leave, walked on until we reached China. By then we were a disorganised rabble and I had even lost my remaining trunk. This gave me problems when I reached Shanghai, but I found a way to earn a little money for clothes and food, so managed to survive.'

This catches my attention. 'What did you do?' I asked.

She shrugs.

'Managed. I met some friends who helped me in several ways and one kind gentleman eventually brought me to London where I found you, my dear little friend. And here we are living happily on the money remaining from my darling Grand Duke's fortune that your English government so kindly recovered from those disgusting communistic Russians. We live well now, don't we?'

'We certainly do.'

At that moment I decide not to shoot or strangle her the next time she calls me "Little Man."

If I do, those disgusting Russians may reclaim her cash and I will no longer be able to enrich myself by moving lumps of her cash to my own accounts.

I suppose, on reflection, it is better to count the blessing of being so close Madame Sinskaya's, bank balance, rather than keep complaining.

Timmy – Aged Seven

Why is Mum shouting at me to get up? She's such a bully. I don't want to go to school. I like it here in bed. My Mum is so cruel. She makes me eat peas. She knows I hate peas, but she always makes me eat them. And she makes me clean my teeth twice a day. I don't know why I have to clean them in the evening, when I cleaned them in the morning. And I don't like that squidgy white toothpaste. Why can't I have green stuff like Billy at school? He says it tastes lovely and makes lines and patterns on the towel.

And she makes me have a bath every day, when I am still clean from the bath I had yesterday. And she keeps pushing my head under water. She says she is washing my hair, but I think she is trying to drown me for the insurance, like that lady on television the other night. I'm not sure what insurance is, but that lady got lots of money, although she ended up in jail at the end. I don't want my Mum in jail, but I'll get her sent there if she keeps ducking me under water.

My Mum just doesn't understand me. She never listens to what I tell her. Nor does my Dad. He tells silly jokes all the time and thinks he's so funny. He tells them to my friends at the school gate and rolls about laughing. We have to laugh too, although his jokes are always the ones told us yesterday. And last week. He's so embarrassing.

At football he keeps shouting and telling me what to do. He always complains about the referee. So do all the other Dads. One lady said she comes because they're better entertainment than the game. My Dad never shouts at anyone on Sports Day. Mum says it's because he is too busy watching the older girls running and jumping. He says, 'What nonsense,' but Mum is right. I see him looking at the fifth and six year girls, with their long legs and bouncy bits. Most of the other Dads do too. I think they're silly.

Mum is still calling from the kitchen. 'If you don't get up soon Timmy, you won't be able to have breakfast.'

See if I care. She doesn't give me the right things to eat for breakfast anyway. She makes me eat porridge and bits of fruit cut up in a bowl or cornflakes with no sugar. Why can't I have proper like food like Billy at school? Like burgers, pizza and fish fingers. Or those chicken nuggets. I've told my Mum and she told Billy's Mum and made her angry said 'He's always inventing stories. Of course I don't give him burgers and things for breakfast.'

He says I got him into trouble and wouldn't speak to me for two days. He's older than me and when we were speaking again, said his mother made that up because it is her business what she gives him for breakfast. I told my Mum, but it made no difference. She kept on with porridge and things. She is so unfair.

She's still shouting at me to get up, so I suppose I'd better. 'You'll be late for school,' she says. What do I care? I don't like school. They never tell me anything interesting that will help me be a pop star or an astronaut. I'd make a good pop star. But I think I'll be an astronaut. It's easy. I've seen Mr Spock on television. He just floats around and goes on planets and tells people what to do. I'd be good at that. I wonder if being in space gives you funny ears? Perhaps I'll be a footballer. They don't get funny ears.

And at school the silly new girl called Minnie keeps trying to kiss me. Her face is all spotty and I don't like her. Mind you I felt upset when I saw her trying to kiss Billy as well. He says he doesn't mind the spots. So he's silly too.

Another thing about school. They make me work so hard I think I should be paid. Grownups get paid for working and I know that lots of them don't work as hard as me.

My Mum is still shouting and is starting to sound angry. I know she'll make me eat porridge, then my Dad will tell me silly jokes in the car and when we get to the school gate he'll get out and tell the same jokes to the other boys and go across and talk to Billy's Mum. He does it every morning. He leans close and whispers. She puts a hand over her mouth and giggles. Every single morning. Perhaps I should tell Mum.

In school they'll waste my time with all those silly lessons. They never tell me anything to help me be the captain of a big ship or a fighter pilot. And Billy will poke my ribs and tell me he kissed Minnie again. I hate Billy.

I think I'll have to call that telephone line and tell them at how badly I'm treated. They'll send the police round at breakfast to make Mum give me proper food. And they'll stop my Dad telling silly jokes. I won't tell them about Billy's Mum and how Dad makes her giggle, but I'll get him into trouble for letting my Mum drown me because she wants the insurance.

Or perhaps I'll just run away.

Then they'll all be sorry.

A Secret In The Family

My Mother sent me up in the attic to find a box of Christmas decorations. 'It's in the far-left hand corner,' she said. 'Don't tear that nice skirt on a nail.'

Behind the Christmas box I found a tattered old carton, falling apart on one side. It must have been there for years, unseen in the weak light from a small electric bulb.

I dragged it out, making sure not to push my fingers through the rotten cardboard. When I placed it on the carpet beside the decorations, one side collapsed. Papers, letters and photographs spilled onto the carpet.

Mother turned pale. Tears, quickly suppressed, passed through her eyes. With a sharp gasp, she said 'Oh. I thought your father had burnt that years ago.'

I reached out.

'Stop,' she snapped. 'Not until I'll tell you what's in there.'

I sat for the next hour, listening.

'We never told you about your Great Uncle Eric. Those papers are the story of his life. He turned out to be a little devil as a boy. Always in trouble at school, always pinching things from houses and shops, always without punishment, whatever he did.

Because as well as being a clever spinner of lies and excuses, he had a handsome little face, a lovely smile and a beautiful voice. From the age of seven, you'd look at this little angel and believe every fib, every tall tale and every false story.

By the age of seventeen he had become an expert con man able to wheedle anything he wanted out of young girls or young women. Fathers and young men would come knocking and leave blaming their daughters or girlfriends for seducing this innocent young fellow. Some of the older ones even paid him money to keep quiet.

At the age of twenty, his university dons, too intelligent to be taken in, threw him out. Completely sure of his charm, good looks and the ability as an expert forger picked up from one of the art lecturers, he started to roam the world.

Stories kept coming back about him. He spent a short time in an American jail after convincing a hospital with self-written medical qualifications from the non-existent University of Budleigh Salterton. His complete incompetence caused them to check a map and discover the town did not exist in the Hebrides, but in Devon. He charmed a female judge into a light sentence. When released he had an affair with the poor woman and escaped to Mexico with her bank balance.

Flush with money, he married three women over a period of six months, omitting to mention his married state to wives two and three, while pledging a life of love and piety in quick succession. All three, rich, middle aged, and susceptible to a handsome young man and a winning smile, found their cash went with him when he skipped the marital home.

Wife one sent her brothers after him; but he had long gone by the time they even started.

In Spain a husband, home early one afternoon, found his wife in flagrante delicto with the washing machine repair man. Uncle Eric got away by diving through a window, grabbing his underpants as he went. He rushed down the road, waving the underpants and screaming. A passing policeman knocked down and arrested the wronged husband for threatening a member of the public.

We don't know how Uncle Eric managed after that one. Perhaps some middle-aged lady, having seen what he certainly had to offer, took him in. There is no doubt he would have taken her in and moved on with her worldly goods as soon as he had assessed and counted them.

The next we heard is that he took a job as accountant in an African diamond mine. This would be right up his street, except he had no head for figures. He couldn't count beans, let alone money. He could certainly count diamonds and turned up in Amsterdam selling handfuls with beautifully forged certificates of origin.

He would have been able to retire on the fortune he should have made, but his poor head with figures extended to date. The documents had apparently been signed, stamped and authenticated on the eleventeenth of Octember 1795. Those little bits of paper landed him in a Dutch prison.

Your father sent him a letter, but Uncle Eric didn't take kindly to instructions and forgiveness from a priest. He telephoned from jail and pretended to be someone else, although Dad knew his voice.

After his escape made him famous we were able to follow his trail in newspapers and magazines, with stories of exploits in the Caribbean and then to South America, where the trail went cold and so did he. We think he fell out with a drugs cartel.

Your father tried to find out where they buried him but went to heaven in sorrow that he could not pray over Uncle Eric's grave, or, perhaps, the mound of dirt Eric arranged, no doubt with a beautiful headstone telling us what a fine and honest fellow he had been..

Now I've told you, take that damned box and burn it. But not until after you've read all your Uncle Eric's letters, photos and newspaper cuttings. The damned man sent them to us, thinking we should be proud of what he called his career and the film Hollywood made about him.

Promise me you'll destroy the box and everything in it then forget him. I want nothing of Uncle Eric left. Not a hint of ash. Not a scrap of partly burnt paper.

The awful thing is, he's been such a clever cheat all his life, I wouldn't be surprised if he walked through the door right now.

In case that happens, think you should know that Uncle Eric is your real father.'

Five Minutes

One cold and misty November evening I entered my London Club and found it quiet and empty.

'Probably the weather, Sir,' said the concierge. 'Sir William is alone in the library with his brandy. He'll probably welcome company. What can I bring you?'

'I'll have a brandy too, thanks.'

Concierge took my heavy coat and I found Sir William deep in one of those soft leather chairs that are part of the uniform of such clubs, along dim lights.

'Ha, Smith. Glad to see you. Is Smith your real name?'

'It's the one I use, Sir Henry. It does the job. Simple and easy to remember,'

'Yes. Of course. Best to be simple in your line of trade.'

My brandy arrived. I sipped and looked at Sir William, apparently deep in thought, a slender finger stroking his silken moustache.

'Are you thinking through a difficult diplomatic conundrum?' I asked.

'No. I'm thinking of a phrase I read many years ago. Someone had written, 'In five minutes Kings can be dead and Kingdoms changed."

'I suppose that's true. A bullet. The slash of a knife or sword. Dead king. Long live the next one.'

'My thoughts are on a different kind of five minutes, old boy. No bullets. No swords. Just a simple ordinary mistake. So simple you would, in normal times, never notice it.'

'Do tell,' I said.

'In the closing years of the war, we sent a very clever and beautiful young woman to Paris with the perfect cover of an Indian princess and the task of setting up a special network composed only of young women. She thought up the idea and planned to use only high born ladies to squeeze information from colonels and above. Those were the johnnies who knew it all.'

'Brilliant.'

'Yes. As an idea. But we were not sure of it succeeding in practice. We tried to dissuade her, but she determined to go ahead and do her bit. She already knew all the top officers in our own forces and realised that when faced with a good-looking girl, all powder and paint, a sweet smile and a willing ear, even the most guarded of officers let all sorts slip in an effort to impress.'

'Did it work?'

'We never knew. Having been brought up in France she had the language to perfection, including the Parisian accent and all the current slang and fashion. Even the most French of Frenchmen would never have twigged. She breezed through all the training, fantastic memory, tough as any man in combat training.

Could out-walk and out-climb most of the fellows across swamps, up cliffs or mountains and the hardships of survival training never gave her a moment of distress on land or sea.'

'She sounds perfect. What went wrong?' I asked.

'The stupidest little thing. Something in no training manual. I took full responsibility and resigned. She arrived safely in Paris on a beautiful sunny day. Went to the apartment her family had owned for centuries and instead of waiting for Jean-Pierre our Station Chief, freshened up and went for a walk along the boulevards.'

I said, 'She broke protocol. She should have waited.'

'Exactly. Jean-Pierre arrived exactly on time, saw her a hundred meters away and followed. He watched her pass several cafes before settling at a table next to four Gestapo officers drinking wine. Naturally they eyed her up. Any man would. A pretty woman shining in the sun.'

'When do the five minutes come in?'

'Now. She ordered tea and a small jug of milk. Not quite normal in a Paris pavement café, but not too abnormal to be an error. In the four minutes before the tea arrived, one of the German officers engaged her in conversation. When the tea arrived, she took the tiny jug and poured milk followed by the tea.'

'Wait.' I said. 'That's not the way the French do it.'

'Exactly. They pour tea then milk. On the fifth minute Jean-Pierre saw the officer she'd been chatting with stand and with a perfectly polite bow and say, 'Mademoiselle, I must ask you to come with us. It is my duty to arrest you.'

'Jean-Pierre, greatly distressed, watched our Princess climb into a staff car, her bright hair reflecting the sun. We later heard that, although tortured, she revealed nothing of our training or methods. They took her first to Sachsenhausen, then to Belsen. As soon as I heard we'd taken the place I rushed to Germany, hoping to bring her home, but she died of cholera two days before our Army arrived.'

'How terrible. How utterly awful.'

'Yes. I tried my best to stop her from going. In the hour before she boarded that tiny 'plane, I took her privately to my office to tell her how much I loved her and begged, hugging and kissing her, almost weeping at her proud insistence fighting in some way for the two countries to which she owed so much.'

'You were in love with her?

No. Not in love. I loved her as a father loves his only daughter.'

'Your daughter? You sent your daughter to France?'

'Yes, I did. In the end I saw it as my duty. I knew she may be captured, tortured and probably shot. But I did it, never knowing that five minutes and a little drop milk would be the end of her.

The Most Important Train in History

Zurich – April 1916

In his cramped study, Lenin sat scribbling an angry note, instructing Trotsky to stop wasting time and get on with pushing the Bolsheviks into a majority in Parliament. 'Once you have done this we can infiltrate and overthrow the government,' he wrote, spots of ink splashing from his pen nib at its speed of passage across the paper. 'Don't waste time. Act now. Let me know your detailed plan.'

A tap at the door.

'Come in,' he shouted. 'Hurry. I'm busy.'

His wife, obviously nervous at breaking the strict rule that he must never be disturbed, stepped halfway into the untidy room.

'Three gentlemen to see you Vladimir Ilyich,' she whispered.

'Show them in, show them in.'

He turned his letter to Trotsky over but made no attempt to tidy the piles of papers on his desk. Nor did he stand to welcome or shake hands with the three who stepped in.

'Sit down, sit down,' he snapped. 'I've been expecting you.'

He started across the desk at the two Germans, both dressed in the formal dark suits and stiff collars of senior diplomats. Lenin nodded at the

Swiss communist who had negotiated this meeting and said, 'Well?'

'Herr Lenin,' said one of the Germans. 'We have arranged for your return to Russia.'

'How?'

'Your Swiss friend here has persuaded us that your opposition to the war means your return will be good for Germany. He tells us you will remove Russian armies from the Eastern Front, allowing us to turn all our effort against the British and the French. We plan to take you from Switzerland and across Germany in a sealed train designated as German territory. This means you cross frontiers privately. We have arranged safe passage through Sweden to the north, where you can cross into Finland and reach Petrograd using the Russian rail system.'

'Who pays?'

'The German government.'

'Will my carriage have a samovar? I cannot travel without tea.'

'That can be arranged.'

'I'll let you know tomorrow.'

A few days later Lenin led his wife and thirty other Russian revolutionaries into a specially guarded train at Zurich station, waving his arms and, 'Hurry. The sooner you're aboard, the sooner you'll be in Petrograd.'

Apart from his wife, Lenin hated all the other passengers, who spent their eight days journey to

Petrograd, arguing the finer points of Russian politics, with no thought of any action to take over their homeland. Seated with his wife in an end compartment near the samovar, with an exercise book balanced on his knee, he wrote in his usual furious fashion, views, ideas, speeches and plans on how to take over Russia.

Rolling across the German countryside, Lenin observed and pointed out to his wife the complete absence of young men in villages they passed. 'All at the front or dead,' he said, realising that the Germans, who had looked at him with such contempt in Zurich, almost certainly needed him more than he needed them.

Reaching the Baltic, a Swedish ferry took Lenin and his party on a stormy crossing to Trelleborg and, under German diplomatic protection, by train and bus to northern Sweden and the border with Finland. Snow still lay thick on the ground and on the Torne River bridge, so they clambered into horse-drawn sleds and entered Russian controlled Finland.

'We may be turned back or arrested,' Lenin warned his fellow travellers. Instead, they were met by the Russian revolutionary and bank robber Josef Stalin and a few other senior Bolsheviks. Lenin felt his distrust of Stalin rise to rage, but his inscrutable lizard eyes showed no hate and he allowed the man to join him on their two-day train journey to Petrograd.

The wretched third-class carriages made the German train seem luxurious, but, although he showed it to no-one, Lenin felt ecstatic at seeing Russian soldiers and peasants, knowing that he had returned to save them from an oppressive and chaotic Social Democrat government.

On the night of April 6th, 1917, Lenin arrived at the Finland Station in Petrograd, to a muted welcome from a group of Bolsheviks he could see were, worried by this surprise return to his homeland.

Word must have gone around the city earlier of his imminent arrival, for he saw an excited crowd pushing and shoving in the arrival hall.

He strode from the platform, hopped onto a luggage trolley, swept off his felt cap and started the speech that changed the world.

He Lost It

Professor Sir Henry Watkins, eminent psychiatrist, sat in his consulting room sipping tea and reading a newspaper story. Apparently, a young man stepped onto an underground train carrying what seemed to be a long flute case. He travelled for five stations and left the train minus his case.

A few minutes later the young man appeared on CCTV, jumping on and off trains, rushing around passenger corridors and platforms, grabbing passers-by in obvious panic, in what seemed to be a frantic search for his flute.

Half an hour later, the young man threw himself into the path of the two o' clock arrival at Bond Street.

Sir Henry reflected for a moment on this sad case. Surely the young fellow could have waited and gone to Lost Property.

Ah well.

His intercom whispered that his next appointment had arrived.

He folded the newspaper and stood, brushing crumbs of a recent biscuit from his lap, and caught sight of himself in the wall mirror, placed carefully so he could admire himself and confirm what a fine fellow he looked.

The expensive suit and matching waistcoat; the perfectly knotted tie and stiff white collar, the mane of beautiful white hair sweeping back from a noble brow. Oh, what the perfect combination of knighthood and medical knowledge. He loved to see his patients relax the moment they walked through the door.

Not so this new fellow, scuttling through, head down, fingers twisted and pulling at each other in the classic indication of extreme distress.

He gave only a short glance at the magnificent Sir Henry and threw himself onto the leather couch by the bookcase without being directed or invited. He sat in complete silence; head bowed.

Sir Henry shrugged, walked round the desk to his special chair and sat in front of this poor wretch.

'I need you to speak to me,' said Sir Henry in his deliberately low soothing voice. 'Otherwise, I cannot help you.'

'He lost it,' said the new patient.

'Lost what?'

'I cannot tell you.'

'You must tell me something or we shall have thirty costly minutes of silence. Please tell me why you are here.'

'Because he lost it.'

'Lost what?'

'I cannot tell you.'

Sir Henry sighed and in a sharp voice snapped, 'Look at me.'

The new patient's whole body twitched.

For a second, he looked up.

Just enough time for Sir Henry to snap his fingers and hypnotise the fellow with an abrupt command.

It always works.

Catch their eyes with his Rasputin stare and click the thumb and first finger and off they go.

Sir Henry delved into the man's mind and background as best he could but discovered little. The idiot kept repeating he mantra, 'He lost it,' without telling what had been lost.

By careful digging Sir Henry mined deeply enough to discover the patient and the dead young man were connected, but in what way he could not bring out.

In the end he gave up, planted a few happy thoughts in his patient's mind and lifted him slowly from his deep trance.

The happy thoughts seemed not to work very well.

With a hand on the poor chap's slumped shoulder, Sir Henry guided him out to Miss Smith, waited long enough to see her extract a tidy fee from the fellow and gave the incident no more thought.

Until the next morning when two serious-looking men arrived without appointment waving warrant cards, insisted on seeing him and quite literally, forced their way into the consulting room and placed themselves on the two chairs facing Sir Henry's shining dark-wood desk.

'Are you police?' asked Sir Henry.

'No.'

'What are you then? And why have you come here in this rather rude manner?'

In the moment of silence that followed, Sir Henry ran his eyes over his visitors. Both in almost identical pinstripe suits, white shirts; what could be regimental ties and highly polished black shoes. Both with blank eyes and even blanker faces, they could have been manufactured from the same mould.

'We belong to the security services,' said one.

'Which security service?'

'We cannot tell you,' said the other

'Are you here about the gentleman who consulted me yesterday?'

'Yes.'

'Well. I can't help you. He couldn't tell me anything either.'

'On behalf of the government we demand that you tell us what he said.'

'Not a word. Doctor and patient security, I'm afraid.'

'He must have said something.'

'He walked in and said, "He lost it." That is all I can say of his visit.'

'Lost what?'

'He never said. Nor did he say who lost it.'

They frowned in unison.

One said, 'We know he consulted with you for thirty minutes. If you refuse to give us information you will be placed under arrest and held at a secret location until we receive a full and frank statement of all he told you.'

Sir Henry stood and aimed his fiercest Rasputin stare into their eyes.

They stared back in that official high-ranking civil servant way of the completely confident government servant.

Sir Henry clicked his fingers and off they went, heads dropping back, eyes closed.

Sir Henry chuckled and by the time he finished, the first man woke with a happy smile, the second with sparkling eyes as though expecting some great event.

Both stood and shook hands, thanking Sir Henry for his co-operation and courtesy.

'Please let me know if there is more can do,' he said, ushering them out.

From his window he watched them walk down Harley Street, knowing that by the time they reached the corner they would have forgotten everything except what he had planted in their minds.

He turned away chuckling and caught sight again of the handsome reflection staring back from his mirror.

He winked at himself and sat down.

He pressed the intercom button.

'A cup of tea, please, Miss Smith. And two biscuits from that special caddy you have tucked away.'

J Newton IIIA (Written in 1948 at the age of 11.)

The Curse

Jim Dawson stated up from where he lay, in his quiet village home in Somerset. The thud of horses hooved on hard earth and the hoarse shouting of the town crier startled him. He ran out onto the road and saw a group of men hustling and jostling round the crier. The latter shouted to them to give him room and with a sweep of his arm set his bell aringing. "Oyes, Oyes, Oyes", he cried unrolling a huge parchment. "The renowned Sir Francis Drake, who sailed round the world and into Cadiz Harbour to sink many ships and kill many Spaniards requests that the men of England should listen. The aforesaid has reason to believe that the Spanish are building a great fleet for the purpose of attacking our fair land of England and he requests that the men of this hamlet who have been to sea before to come to Plymouth Harbour and sign on his ships to beat those Spanish invaders." Jim walked away from the hubbub that had arisen, thinking deeply.

Three days late, Jim was trudging along the dusty English road. He was going to join Sir Francis Drake in Plymouth Harbour. It was just a day since he had made up his pack, kissed his mother goodbye down and walked away down the road towards Devon.

Jim walked across Somerset, through the Blackdowns and was crossing the border into Devon when the thud of horses' hooves thundered behind him and made him look up. An old farm cart was rattling behind him at a terrific pace, drawn by two thoroughbreds of fine mettle galloping along so fast that it looked as if the cart would fall to pieces.

It did. One of the wheels stuck a stone and the cart just collapsed. Jim ran back to help the driver, "A woman," he gasped and redoubled his efforts to rescue her from under the beam from which she was pinned.

Another heave, a groan from underneath, and the beam was off. Jim dragged it to the side and ran back to carry the old woman to the greasy wayside bank.

He looked at the old woman and saw that she was dying. Her eyes were fluttering and her breath came in quick short gasps. She opened her eyes. "What happened?' she said. "To Plymouth Harbour to join Sir Francis Drake," her replied. "You're too late," she said. "The English fleet is sailing into battle now My son Harry is aboard one of the ships."

Suddenly she gave an awful scream. "My son," she cried. "My son has just been shot by one of the Spanish sharpshooters".

'A soothsayer!" gasped Jim, "A Witch!" Witches wee much feared then. The old woman seemed to go into a trance; her face lit up with a strange light. "Wind rain and waves," she said in a soft low voice. "Wind rain and waves," her voice rose into a high pitched scream. "Sweep these foreign murderers away from our shores. Wreck them on the coasts of Scotland, Ireland, France and England. Kill them, kill them, Kill them." With one last scream of wild laughter she fell back and died.

Jim looked round him in wonder. The sky was darkening, the wind was rising, driving rain and hail before it.

He buried the old woman by the tree under which she had died. When he looked for the horses they were gone. Only the wreck of the cart told the tale of what had happened. Jim turned, and slowly trudged towards Plymouth and shelter.